Sometimes A River Song

Avril Joy

About the Author

Avril Joy was born in Somerset, the setting for her first novel, *The Sweet Track* (Flambard Press, 2007). Her short fiction has appeared in literary magazines and anthologies including Victoria Hislop's *The Story: Love, Loss & the Lives of Women: 100 Great Short Stories*, and has been shortlisted for awards including the Bridport, the Manchester Prize for Fiction and the Raymond Carver Short Story Prize. In 2012 she won the inaugural Costa Short Story Award. Before becoming a full-time writer Avril worked as a teacher and manager in the women's prison, HMP Low Newton. She lives with her partner in County Durham and blogs regularly about writing and life at www.avriljoy.com

Published by Linen Press, Edinburgh 2016
1 Newton Farm Cottages
Miller Hill
Dalkeith
Midlothian
EH22 1SA

www.linen-press.com

A CIP catalogue record for this book is available from the British Library.

Cover photograph: © arcangel-images.com
Cover design: Louise Santa Ana / Katie Joy / Zebedee Design, Edinburgh
Typeset in Sabon by Zebedee Design, Edinburgh
Printed and bound by Lightening Source

ISBN 9780957596801

Acknowledgements

My heartfelt thanks go to my editor, Lynn Michell, for her belief in me and in the story. I am grateful for her support, guidance and astute editing which have helped make this book the best it can be. Likewise I am indebted to Liz Rao, assistant editor, for working assiduously and enthusiastically alongside us.

My thanks, as always, to Wendy Robertson for starting me on this road. Thank you, Wendy, for all the days spent writing together, for your wisdom and for our enduring friendship. Thank you, Gillian, for journeying with us.

I am grateful to photographer and writer, Chris Engholm and to Gayne Preller for their tireless work on the Hugo and Gayne Preller's *House of Light* Exhibition which inspired my floating photographic studio and also for our correspondence.

Many thanks to my family. To John for being my first reader, to Katie for working her magic on the cover. To my father, Patrick, and to David for their unquestioning support.

For my brother and for Jan

River in our blood. Ain't nothing we can do about it. Ain't nothing even if we be minded which we ain't seeing as river be our blood, our breath, our being too. River our country, our voice. Loud in the fossil mountains where the bobcats hide and it go rushing over rock and boulder, past clay Bluff and willow bar, through hickory and pine. Hush when it get to wandering in the grass and the cotton fields, grow fat and lazy like the silver eel. River always changing. Never still.

Winter come, it be the colour of fishes' skin, hiding in ice. We hiding too, coats and quilts, and wind from the north eating our bones. Spring be green of leaf and blossom, blue smoke rising from the burning prairie and we all out fishing and planting. Come summer, river shrink, mayfly and mosquito swarm. No one walking barefoot for fear of snakes and everyone praying for rain. Autumn follow in mist, hang like a spirit on the water.

River bind and shape us all, body and soul. River the skin we wear. We swimming in its pools, roaming in forest and swamp. Know its every mood, every whisper. Haunting in the ghost tree, bark of the mud cat, cry of the lone wolf. River fever be our fever. River thirst, our mouths dry, and we all praying for a hard rain. River be one of us. Live beside it and live on it. River our home, only home we know.

There be a dozen or so boats, moored in the Creek. River rats is what the townsfolk call us and they don't mean good by it.

Even though we be their white brothers and sisters they call us low down, crawling, because we ain't sleeping and waking and eating and living on dry land. They forgetting there be work on the water, diving and mussel hauling, button factory and cannery. There be hunting and fishing, packing in ice, timber rolling and logging, barges and paddle steamers. But right now with the land turning to dust around us, the crops failing and folk going hungry, when there be no work, and they say we be passing through a great depression, river look like the best place to be.

Boat rest on the cypress logs, drift and bob with the current that come up Creek. Morning, wake to dawn light, brush of oar on water, soft splash of the jumping bullfrog, songbird and dragonfly skittering across the sky. Night fall, day drain from the world, stars spill and vapours rise. We sleep to the lull and rock of moving water, think on the journey, source to sea. Think on the new day. For there always be a new day.

River don't run in a straight line, ain't one thing forever. It change course, make itself over. Always moving on. Bringer of life, taker of life. We born on the river and we die by the river. That's what daddy say. I belong to the river and I belong to him and he will do with me as he see fit.

1

It happens when I am just a crawling child, one week past my first birthday and I up and crawl right off the boat. Least, that's what mama say. She call out, 'Aiyana,' but I already under. Gone. Breathing that thick, brown river water. He pull me out like he do the snapping turtle because daddy a man of river ways. I blue, mama says. He thump my chest good and hard and some of the river come up and some stay put. They say is a miracle that I'm alive.

After, I turn to a sickly child with coughs and fevers and bruises and boils, river water still in me. Always. Nights I feel it, river suck at my throat. I am spluttering and choking like a chicken for the pot. Hetty, she be my sister, she shaking me, tell me I gotta wake up, be calm now and find my breath.

There five of us children living on the boat with mama and daddy. Hetty, she the eldest, she sixteen, then me fifteen, then Lyle, ain't hardly a year between each of us, and then the twins Eugene and Albert, they come late. All mama's time taken up with keeping us clean, with cooking and washing, and she glad of my help because I stay home. All these years I ain't walking out the Creek to the school house with the others. All these years, mama get sadder and sicker, and I stay with her and do the chores. Make the cornbread and carry the water, wash and clean, see to the chickens, cut the greens, shop and cook. Do as daddy say. According to him I ain't in need of learning. I too sick, too backward, ain't worth it. Ain't worth more than another man's dog, he say. Never know why he hate me so much. Why he want to punish me like he do.

First time I be four and the river be high. He make me kneel and take a hold of my hair. He despise my red hair, say it be the mark of my shame. I so wish it be black like my brothers and sister. He force my head down under the water and hold it there. My lungs fill, ready to burst, stomach rocking, dark world closing in. When he let me up, I gasping like a fish on dry land. He don't even look, he walk away like it be nothing. Swear, one day the river gonna take my life. I thinking, he hold me back down one more time and I be gone.

He ain't done it for a while now, not since the time last fall. That time, the blackness close in around me. When he finish and he let me up I fighting for my breath. I lie there and I lie there but it don't come. Hetty lift my head in her lap. Mama say Lyle gotta fetch Doctor Miller quick, give me an injection like he do, though I rather the yellow powder he give me when I just small.

Daddy say we ain't got no money to be calling no doctor.

Hetty mad, more than I see ever before. I see it in her eyes. 'That is nonsense,' she say. 'You know fine well the doctor come here and ask for nothing. We are a charity case, God help us. You gotta send for him, else Aiyana she gonna die right before your very eyes. I swear no child of mine is ever gonna want for no doctor. I swear no child of mine ever gonna have a father like you. You ain't a father and that is a fact.'

Daddy step towards her but she don't move, like she saying, 'Come on then, do your worst, I daring you,' and I see there something between them more than my lungs. She been angry with him since way back when and I reckon it got something to do with the way he always coming to fetch her at night and she always pretending she asleep.

Mama don't say nothing but the twins they set up howling and Lyle he get up and say he going to fetch the doctor and nobody stopping him. Castor, his grizzly old dog, jump up and follow him. My breath fast. Sound like the wind in my chest. I don't speak. Daddy leave.

Doctor Miller come. Look kindly. I ask him for the yellow powder but he shake his head and open up his bag and take out the syringe. He give me the injection and tell mama she gotta call him sooner next time, soon as it start. I feel the blackness come over me but my chest open and my breath come and I know Hetty and Lyle save me.

Hetty ain't got a good word to say about daddy. 'Why do you think everyone on this river is so afraid of Floyd Weir? It's because he don't care who or what he hurt. Look at mama, look what he do to her. The beatings and...' She stop, like she ain't sure what she gonna say next. 'He's got hands that don't know where they belong. He is like the fox in the chicken coop, Aiyana. You wait, you'll see. One night he will come, sure as the fox comes for its supper and...' She stop and sigh 'Soon as I get a house with Johnson,' Johnson be her beau, 'you are leaving here, you will come and live with me.' She say she gonna marry Johnson just as soon as she leave school.

I say, 'I gonna marry December Lutz, he the only man for me. Me and December, we always been sweethearts.'

'You know daddy forbid it, the Klan forbid it. If he ever find out, then most likely he'll take to holding your head under the water and he won't let up. It ain't gonna happen, Aiyana. Not ever.'

'No? Well, just you wait and see.'

No matter what anyone say, no matter what Hetty say or daddy say, I ain't giving up on December. He a woods colt child, born of ice, left frozen and dying in the reeds on the river bank. Hannah Lutz take him in. Daddy say if she'd been minding her own business it had been a better thing, child die and no one know any different. December mixed blood, that's why he left to die. Mixed blood ain't welcome on the river. Klan don't approve. But I glad to my bones Hannah Lutz save him. He

13

my first and only love. I never have another love like December.

We grow up together, what with him being a child of colour, half one colour, half another and not going to school like the others. And me half child, half river, we the same in that respect. I don't see the difference colour make but it sure make a difference to some folk and some folk think it a wicked thing if a white woman or a white man go with a coloured person. Hannah she don't see colour, she just see a frozen child. Got no babies of her own. Mama say only child Hannah Lutz ever have slip from her body, no breath, silent as the silvery fish in the shade of the Bluff. She make a willow cot and send it back to the river.

Cold day, mist hanging on the river. Outside, don't hardly see from one boat to another. Fish jumping and if a person so wants, he catch a whole stringer of catfish and bream on a day like today. Daddy out hunting and mama resting. The others all be at the schoolhouse where I never been. I figure I alone. Boat still in the water, rain on the roof. I on my tiptoes so as not to wake mama. Listen for her sleeping breath, it come slow. I go to the bed. Kneel on the boards by the chest she keep there, gentle so as not to wake her.

It be made of red cedar and carved with angel heads. I smooth my fingers on the angel heads, slide over curls and lips, trace feather wings. Feel for the key, lying underneath. Pull it up from the dust, wipe it clean. Put the key in the lock and turn. Chest open. I lift the lid, and there it be, the book, the book daddy say I be forbidden to touch. Say I ain't good enough to set eyes on. Is black, black bible, corners ragged, back broken. Belong to daddy's daddy who I ain't never seen. Mama say it come across the water, with the family, then handed down. Ask me, is wasted on daddy. He don't ever read it, don't even take it out from the Angel Chest.

It heavy as a rifle. Need two hands to lift. Place it on the floor. Open. Turn it soft pages. It look and feel to me like a

14

perfect thing. Smell of prairie grass and clover. Only trouble be I try to fathom the words but no matter how long I stare they do not show. I am like him hunting in the woods waiting for the rustle of the whitetail in the chinaberries, only nothing come. I do not know the word. The marks stay put. They be as heavy as my heart. They be my tears on the page.

The world be made of the word. How my life gonna be worth anything if I don't read? I ain't settling for just river child. Be looking for more. One day I get new clothes, not hand-me-downs, carry my case and my books, go to my work. But how I gonna get a job if I don't read? How I ever gonna know the bible for myself, the words of the songs and stories? How I gonna teach my children? It be time to stop pretending. Time to find my way out of the darkness and there be only one way.

Only one thing I want more than December and that be schooling. Even though daddy forbid it, I want it bad, wanting like a thorn buried deep under my skin. The more time run away, the more that thorn pinch and prick at me. I gotta have it. Soon. It be my only salvation. I am like mama, she ain't reading either. She say her time to learn be gone now. Ask me, mine be running out fast.

Mama stir. She talking in her sleep. I close the bible. Rest my hand there and wonder why he forbid me a thing of beauty like this. That be when I feel it. Air change, grow thick around me. Hairs on my arms standing up, skin crawl and breath quicken. Smell of sweat and blood in the room. Hunting blood. He come silent as a ghost but I know he be there. Black shadow hanging at the door. I turn and see him. Daddy. He step out of the doorway and come towards me. Got his big skinning knife hanging in his hand.

My hair fall at his feet. Fall on my feet. Lie like red grass on my legs. He do it inside. At the kitchen table. He say, 'You asked for this, child. I forbade you to touch that chest and that bible. This is what comes when you defy me. That book got nothing to do with you and never will have.' Then he call out to mama, 'Here come see, this knife could cut butter, honed it good and proper on that bench stone.' He laugh, tug at my hair, chop, chop with the knife.

Mama stir, come slow into the kitchen then wake fast when she see what he do.'Floyd, God have mercy, what are you doing?' She go to take his arm away. 'In God's name, stop. Floyd. I'm begging you.' He hold the knife up to her. Then push her off with his elbow. When he finish he tell her go fetch the hand mirror, make sure I get a good, proper look at myself. Then he take his knife and he go.

When she see daddy be gone, mama take the hand mirror away. Tell me not to fret, she gonna make my hair nice as she can. I reckon there ain't no mending what he do but I sit and try to catch my breath while she take her sewing scissors and cut. After, she say it ain't so bad. Hair sap your strength and I need all mine on account of my lungs.

Lyle be the first back from school, Castor his dog following on his heels. When he see me he get a shock. He say, 'Jesus Aiyana, what's up with your hair?'

'Daddy cut it,' I say. 'With his big skinning knife.'

He shake his head. He keep shaking it. 'One of these days he's gonna hurt you so bad he gonna kill you. Ain't safe for you here anymore, Aiyana,' he say. Then he turn to Castor, ruffle his back and he whisper. 'Time we were thinking of leaving, dog, and that's a fact.'

Mist gone, pale sun falling, moon rising. Dusk. Cold wind at my neck. Rain still. I tell mama I gonna take the boat and row across to grandma's. She don't stop me. Through the reeds, in the shallows, steady the boat, step in and lift the oars. Row. Rain falling round me in circles like the willow hoop of the dreamcatcher. Listen for the river calling me. Hear its voice in the way it move. Times, like the spring flood it be angry and the waves whip up so thick it run backwards, times like summer mornings it be sweet and slow, barely move, mist rising, river of glass, everything glide and glisten, across the water grandma singing to the corn while she hoe. Times, like now, it be cast down and troubling through the moons of rain and winter. Times the river see what daddy do and it sing my sorrow.

2

Grandma's boat quiet as the Creek on a winter's night, soft owl calling, frozen river, frost stars in the black sky falling on trees, everything hide. Nothing move. Creak of the boat and the cypress logs resting on ice. Wish I live with grandma. I do for a while when granddaddy die. I keep her company but then daddy say I getting too much of her ways and he make me come home.

My mama's mama, she from the northern plains, her people Ojibwe. See the future in dreams and visions. Say one day before long I gotta leave the river. I say that ain't gonna happen. She say she pray for me, she call on the eagle to carry her prayers to the Great Spirit, Gichi Manidoo, keep me from danger. Keep me from daddy. Daddy like the Windigoo, grandma say, come up from the water and eat you alive.

My grandma be the first to name me. When I born she fast and she pray, then she tell them, 'The child will be called Aiyana.' Because I am born when the wild plum be in flower, under a blossom moon. So many flowers, grandma say, it turn the wild grasses to snow and the river to cloud. That's what Aiyana be. Blossom. Blossom of the wild plum that grow by the river. I am wild plum, my roots always walking to water.

Her boat small and she paint it yellow. Look like it growing through the willow, sit in the reeds like a yellow siskin. Paint peeling. She don't look after it so good now granddaddy gone.

Now he gone she pining for the north. She ask how come she this far from her people?

She waiting for me. Hear me come even if she don't see me, she standing there, peering out at me. Like she don't know who I be. Got a rusty hanging lamp at her feet and a gun in her hand, belong to granddaddy. When he alive he the best white hunter and trapper this side of the line, catch anything that move, snakes and all, gar and turtle, sell the skins and shell. She got his guns and she liable to go firing them when she feel like it. Got the habit shoot first, think last. Say one day, when he ain't looking, my daddy Floyd might just come in her sights. I don't think she mean it though but it sure do make folks wary. Mostly she shoot the birds from the corn but sometimes she miss and one time she shoot one of the Hartley boys and it take all Lyle's persuading for them not to come looking for her. Daddy cross the river to her boat then, which be a rare thing and he take her gun away from her. Somehow she always find another.

Now things a whole lot worse and she don't see so good, especially in the morning when she wake up. She even go shooting at the twins on their way to school, say she be after the bad spirits. Lyle creep in that night, when she sleeping. He take the bullets and put blanks in. Daddy say he see that gun again and he calling Sheriff Harper, don't care she his mother-by-law or not.

'Is that you, Wild Plum?' She call. She put the gun down. Help me out the boat. Lift the lamp from the deck and then she see. Put her hand to my hair. 'My child, who has done this?'

I don't speak. Breath too short. Tears crowd my eyes. Scared if I speak they fall like the rain. Scared I choke.

'Floyd,' she say. She don't need me to tell her what man can do a thing like this to his child. She dry my tears and take me inside. We sit on her bed of furs and she put the bone comb gentle through my hair, fix a strand with turquoise beads and the feather of the owl. Might as well be a country away. River might as well be a mile wide, might as well be the Mississippi, because it a different world here. Our boat all noise and scraping, shouting and telling, until he get the belt out or such, then it all fear and silence, tight mouth, and anger buried deep as a winter turtle. Only trouble with the winter turtle, one day he gonna wake right up out of his sleep and snap back and when he do he ain't letting go.

Grandma tell me lie down while she fix us some sweetgrass and sage tea. When I real sick and my chest like a jack rabbit with its skin pegged out to dry, if daddy be punishing me for not chopping wood to keep the stove in, or opening the chest, or burning the cornbread or such like, she come for me, make me lie down and feed me tea through a straw. Times she burn the sage with cedar to ward off evil. Times she make me put my head over a pot of mint, take in what steam and smoke I can. I easy then. It ain't a cure but it the whisper of breath, river done leave, and breath come if I wait.

I ain't sure what lungs look like exactly but I think mine be pools, got fish swimming back and forth, causing trouble. I wonder one day if them fish just gonna decide they had enough of being all cooped up inside and jump right up my throat and come out my mouth in a stream like the fountain by the courthouse.

When she bring the tea I tell grandma about the fish.

She say, 'Hush, child, that surely is nonsense if ever I heard it. Fish cannot live inside a body, they are of the water, and jumping fish are of the air, like the fowl. We are one with them but they do not live inside us. You do not have the best breathing apparatus; that is all. You are the man who cuts coal with an axe, the child who picks cotton and breathes the dust. And now your hair is shorn and you are wounded.'

'But I ain't breathing no dust.'

'I know that,' she say.

Then I tell her, 'Never mind my wounds, never mind my

hair. I sad it gone but it grow soon enough and there be other things more important. Things I gotta do. I need to go to school with Hetty and Lyle. Even if it just one year. My lungs fine for school. I gotta learn the word. Lyle always been clever and Hetty she the best reader in her class. Twins even though they be a whole heap of trouble now they turned eight, even they reading, and me, I don't read nothing.'

'Me neither, child. But I know how to snare the deer and the rabbit and how to hunt the bird and find water. I can catch the catfish, cure the mink, mend bones that are broken. I know all these things and many more and I can teach you, child. We need no writing, words that are true will sink deep in our hearts.'

I don't say this ain't enough by my reckoning. Don't say nothing. Know fine well it ain't all bad not going to school. No fighting over coats and boots in winter. When everyone gone, put on mama's top coat and tie it up with an old belt so it don't trail. Boots too big but they belong to my granddaddy, got his old socks too, stuff in the toes. Go outside and break the ice on top of the water barrel and fill the pans. Then back out knocking icicles off the roof. They clatter on the deck. I sweep them in the river and if it be frozen they scatter like pond-skaters on the ice.

When my chores finish, make coffee for me and mama and if it ain't too early go across to grandma, break the winter ice as I go. Don't go looking early mornings because she up and out with the dawn. Depending on the season she be out in the woods tracking something, or she hoeing and singing to her corn, collecting wood for the fire, plants for her medicine, peeling bark for her dreamcatchers. Boat hanging full of them. They like cobwebs on a fall morning, all willow and feather.

I don't say it all bad. I don't say nothing.

Grandma look at me hard and say, 'You are more like me than you know, child. I see it every day now that you are grown.' She shake her head. 'He sees it too. He sees the stranger come with the snow goose and the wind from the north.'

'What stranger?' I ask.

'In time you will learn of the stranger. In time, Wild Plum, every woman must make her own path.'

I ain't sure what she mean but I ain't about to ask her. Grandma be known for talking in riddles. Besides I already hear the voice come across the water. Calling out my name. He been drinking I tell by the way his words be lazy and they tangle up. He looking for a dog to kick.

Grandma say, 'Stay here, Wild Plum. If he try to cross I will see him off with your granddaddy's gun.'

I think of Lyle, how he tell me I ain't safe, how he whisper to Castor it be time to go. I sigh, a long breath.

She sees what I be thinking. 'I fear you can never be safe from him now. He holds the anger so deep it is like a swamp sucking at his feet, dragging him under. I see the owl above you in my dreaming, Wild Plum. It is the portent of danger.'

I think I know that danger. I think how all my life be a drowning, only one step away from the boneyard and I wonder, what man want to kill his child? Take her spirit, her soul? What man throw his child in the river and shout, 'Swim.' How come he hate me that much?

The calling and the cursing die away. I tell grandma I be just fine. Row back across the water. Stars hiding, only black night. Rustle of damp leaves. Red bats roosting in the trees. Up on the bank I grab me some straw and go sleep with the chickens. It ain't the first time and I reckon it ain't the last. Is a safe nest. Soft cluck and warm feather. No one look for me here. Not even December.

3

Sunday, but there ain't no preacher, he be away up river. December send a message, say to meet him on the island. Island like the river, always changing. Be a place that come and go. Skinny in the flood. Fat in the drought when the river disappear. Best thing about it though, got bushes and soft grass to hide in. We lie there and we be hidden from view, lost to the world.

'Is that you Aiyana?' He whisper.

I pull the boat up on the bar. Afternoon and near dark already. Time when shadows rule and the moth flies at the flame. I whisper his name. He pull me to him. I see the look on his face when he see my hair. 'Don't say anything,' I say. 'Is done now. Grow back soon enough.'

We lie in the grass, listen for the river flowing round us. I hot wanting his body next to mine. I like the way that make me feel. Is the best feeling I know. He think so too I sure. He lean over and kiss me and inch his body close, so he half on top of me and something stir inside me that make me want more. I know it be the same for him because he put his hand there and touch me and I don't want him to stop but he do.

'I'm sorry,' he say.

'I ain't. What's to be sorry for? I already tell grandma how we meeting. Don't worry she keep our secret. Say a secret ain't worth its name, ain't worth the keeping if the telling don't hurt someone. Besides according to her we ain't doing nothing wrong. I am the age now and we right for each other.' I know what I say be true because when I am with December my breath come easy and I forget everything. Is like we the only ones on the river and the river be ours. Belong to us alone. Forget all the bad things then, like when daddy punish me and hold my head down under the water. December don't forget though. He stroking my hair.

'Some day I'm gonna take your daddy's head and hold it down under the water, and I ain't gonna let it up. No sir. Gonna keep it there. See how he like it. I swear, so help me God.'

I ain't got an answer. Just lie there feel his hands on my head like a healing. Lips on my mouth. I ain't thinking of the bad things. Or about what happen if daddy find out about me and December. Or of how everybody fixing to hurt daddy one of these days. I think only of good things. Wish we could lie like this forever in a place where no one find us. Close his arms round me and I be the meadowlark in her grassy nest. Head in her wing, shelter from the winter cold.

December's arms big and he strong as a gar. Made for winter. He start work now up river, in the Ice House, with our neighbour, Pike Dummond. Pike and Ada our white-hair neighbours. They getting old now and their children gone to California. Pike work in the Ice House. Ada, she grow tomatoes after the man from the government tell her to stop raising corn. He say there be money in tomatoes. Pike take them to the cannery in town.

We don't have nothing much to do with neighbours, excepting Pike and Ada. Daddy say mostly they ain't born of the river and don't properly know its ways or God's. Lyle laugh when daddy say that. Daddy say God here in the mountains and the swallows and the meadowlarks. He hear it like we do, the tears of the Cherokee, the Chickasaw and the Crow. They lay heavy on us, it got so the land too sorry to live on so we took to the water. Hetty say that far in the past and these are modern times. But I believe daddy. I hear it whisper in the reeds.

24

I miss December now he be working. Miss the times when Hannah Lutz, if she in a good mood and she not brooding on something, let us sit in her kitchen a while where it warm. She go off to work in Dalton's dry goods store and leave us be. We sit quiet, play checkers and turn on the radio.

Winter seem long then and we always glad of spring, ice break easy like glass, swallows and cuckoos flying back, heron nesting in the reeds. Leaves on the trees like a cloak that make us invisible. We out on the water in the row boat. We outdoors all the time. Do my chores outdoors, the washing and hanging out, beating the dust from the rugs. December set the lines. I gut the catfish, make the cornbread and cut the greens.

When we finish, everything done, we walk the track to town, meet the others coming back from school. If Pike come by in his old truck, he stop and tell us jump in the back. Come summer, road so dusty we like the old grey ghost by the time we jump out.

We envious when we see they come home with books and all but what with his colour and my lungs we barred. Days I glad of it, fed by Hannah, running wild with December. Days I be glad of him looking out for me when my breath don't come, rubbing my back, stealing a fat watermelon from Agar's field and slicing it up to moon wedges to suck the juices from while we lying quiet in the shade. He even carry me on his back when it the worst, got so little breath I cannot speak. Time I cut my foot on the bear trap and it bleed and bleed and he carry me all the way back to grandma and she stop the blood and dress it up with herbs and such. Days like this I glad I ain't at school.

But it ain't the same now. His time taken up with the Ice House and mine with my new pastime, nobody know about, not even December. When nobody watching, or looking for me I walk out the Creek up river. Hurry down by the button factory, where Hetty gonna work making buttons from mussel shells the divers fetch up from the river mud. I collect the

25

buttons that be thrown out because they ain't perfect, because they ain't all looking exactly the same. Why a thing got to be perfect like that? I ain't for that, for everything and everybody the same, else how I gonna fit, else how all the people living on this river gonna fit? If you ask me, they ain't. And I ain't sold on this idea of perfection. Truly I ain't.

Got me an old cotton bag, fill it most times and when I get back to the Creek, hide it in the bushes. Time come and no one knowing, I taking the buttons to town, sell them at the Store. Don't get much above fifty cents a bag but is all adding up. Who knows one day I find a pearl and that be all the money we need. Plenty of folk here looking for the grit in the mussel that make the thing of beauty. Pearls come in all shape and sizes, colours too like rose and peach and black. They mostly in the shape of a tear. Call them *river tears* and they be our greatest treasure. Some fetching fifty dollars or more, even a thousand and that be a fact.

I saving for when me and December got our own boat. He say one year at the Ice House and he have enough money and Pike gonna help him fetch an old boat from down river that going cheap. He do it up so it be a fine boat and we put it any place we want. He sail it to where daddy don't find us. Only trouble he know every inch of this river from mountain to sea. Far as I can tell ain't no hiding place from Floyd Weir.

4

Wolf Moon waning. River bank empty, dusk hanging like crows in the trees, just me and daddy and he ain't happy. He say I spend too much time with grandma, only he don't call her *grandma*.

'Spend all your time with that lazy squaw when you should be chopping wood. Need all the wood we can get. It be your job to gather and chop. You hear me? Told you often enough but seems like you just don't listen. Seems like you'd rather idle away the time with that crazy old redskin.'

He got me by the arm, look around him, see if we be alone. I wondering where mama is. I praying Lyle or Hetty come. He dragging me to the water's edge. I think my head go under and this time I be gone. Ain't got the strength to resist, my lungs already got the water. My heart fast as the hunted deer. If this be living then swear I rather die.

He drag me into the river, he up to his knees, force me under, icy water like a hammer to my head, fill my nose and ears, blackness coming but then his grip go loose. Head come up. He pull me back. I lying on the grass, river weed stuck at my face, in my hair, coughing, spluttering. Hear a growl. Open my eyes, see Castor. He biting at daddy's ankle and he ain't letting go. Lyle step out of the shadows then and point his rifle at daddy. He call Castor off and he come over and take my arm and I don't see where daddy go but he slink away, like a wild cat lost its prey, and we don't see him, not for supper, not after.

Inside it be peace and warm. Hetty find me dry clothes. Then she help mama cook up the catfish and the collard greens. There be biscuits too and when my breath come I sit at the table, twins on one side, Lyle on the other. And after we eat the catfish and greens we have jelly pie. We all smiling now, even mama. And when we finish and the table be clear, Hetty sing *The Arkansas Traveller* because she have a sweet voice and Lyle, he beat the rhythm with his feet. And when the song be over Eugene and Albert get the catalogue out and show me the pictures.

The first time I know I be different is when I am nine years old and the catalogue come, like it do every year. They call it Sears. Mama say every home across America have one. It have pictures of things to buy and numbers and dollar signs for what they cost. Hetty and Lyle go crazy for it and read out what it say about the things they want. But me, I stay dumb. Wonder how they know what the strokes and lines say. They just some kind of crazy pattern to me and they different from the patterns I know, like the pattern on the leaves, speckles on a bird's egg, clouds in a morning sky. They more like the telegraph wire or the railroad, they straight, they something made, something that just ain't natural to me but they something I gotta know.

I let the twins read me from the catalogue and I feel shame. Shame creep over me like the water over my head. How I gonna do anything, be anything, if I don't learn to read? I look at them and look at me and I know I ain't going to school. It be too late for that. I make up mind gotta ask Hetty. Tonight, when we be in bed, I gonna beg Hetty for her help. Offer her the money I been saving from the buttons, give her everything I got, only trouble be that don't amount to anything to speak of, but there gotta be something she want or something I can do for her.

When the dishes done, I go out to lock up the chickens. Lyle follow me.

'It's time to think of going, Aiyana. The weather changing and you gotta be gone by summer. Got no choice. He's gonna kill you for sure. Look what happened today. What if I hadn't come back then?'

'No. I ain't just leaving you all, leaving my home, leaving December. And where to? Besides you forgot? I don't even read. How I gonna make my way? Is not possible.'

'You stay here and you die and that's the truth. He always had it in for you right from when we were small. I know, I hear things Aiyana.'

'What, what things?'

'Hear him say you ain't no child of his and never will be. Hear him tell mama she gotta give you away.'

'No, it ain't true. He don't say that.'

'True or not, that is exactly what he say. Time you started listening. You gotta leave, Aiyana, but you ain't gonna be alone. Me and Castor, we're leaving too.'

I don't say no more, just think about the river and Lyle saving me. Think how one day maybe a bullet find its way to Floyd Weir's heart. Just hope it ain't gonna be a bullet from Lyle's gun.

We go back inside. Still no sign of daddy. Lyle sit by the stove with mama and Castor. Twins already asleep in their kitchen bunks. Hetty say she tired and she going to bed. I say I tired too and I follow her.

Now she grown and daddy don't come for her no more, Hetty getting strong. She know what she want and she make sure she get it. She the only one he don't take the belt to now. She refuse it. A while back I hear her tell him the belt be barbaric. That be a new word to me. Is a new word for him too, I reckon. She say he ain't civilised, that beating be vulgar and cruel and she ain't taking it. It stop him in his tracks and by the time he get to thinking and lifting the belt she gone, and when she come back she got Johnson with her. According to Hetty, Johnson start an argument in an empty house. He

29

big too. Bigger than daddy and daddy don't say nothing.

Hetty and me in bed, lying side by side, boat rocking gentle in the night, I ask her how barbaric spell. What it letters look like. 'Write it for me,' I say.

She turn up the oil lamp, reach for her school book and pencil and she write the letters, b-a-r-b-a-r-i-c.

It look like a fine word to me. It look strong, like a word I need to know. 'I gotta learn how to read, Hetty. I gotta learn before it be too late. I am as fierce as you when it come to reading. I know it gonna be my future. Have to be. Is like my breath, without it I die. I am fixing to learn no matter what it take. Only I can't see a way, can't see how I gonna learn if you ain't helping me. You gotta, Hetty.'

She turn to me and I see she looking hard in my eyes. Looking to see if I mean what I say.

'Please. I ain't gonna be the one who look at the sign in the Store, or the catalogue, or the poster they nail on the fence post and the cottonwoods telling of the preachers, the shows, what coming, what about to happen, I ain't gonna be the one who see them, who see a whole library full of books, just waiting to be open, and not know what they say. You gotta help me. You my only hope, Hetty. I gotta start now. Tonight. First thing you gotta tell me, what they call the letters, when they all put together? I hear the twins saying them over like they be the words to a song, sound like the dancing string on a paper kite.'

'Call it the alphabet.'

'Then you gotta teach me the alphabet, Hetty. Please, I'm begging you. I wash your clothes, iron your dress before you go dancing, before you meet Johnson. Put your hair in rags. I do anything. Give you everything I got. One letter each night. Start now. I got paper I been hiding under the bed, got a pencil too.' I climb out of bed and reach under and bring up a flour sack, take out the old notebook I find on the roadside a month back. It got pages torn and missing but it still paper.

'Alright,' say Hetty and she take the paper from me and she write A, and then beside it she write a. 'This is the first letter A. Big A, and this is small a, you need to know both.'

'I know A. Only thing I do know. Big and small, is in my name.'

'That's right. Copy it down then.'

I copy her letters.

'It makes different sounds,' she say. 'Sometimes it sounds like its name, sometimes it sounds like the a in apple.'

I lie back and say the name and the sounds over and over until I fall asleep. It be the first thing I think of when I wake.

Nights, she teach me. Sometimes more than one letter, and Hetty, she say I learn fast. Before we know it we get to M. M the night Silas come. That the night everything change. After that, no more letters. After Silas come, Hetty forget all about the alphabet.

5

Daddy taken up with the men from the city banks, rich men and the like. Take them out on fishing trips. He say folk stupid enough to pay someone to show them what their ancestor knew fine well, he stupid enough to take it. Only daddy ain't stupid, not when it come to money. According to grandma it rule him and that a bad thing, is what make a man forget his duty to family and nature, she say. Is what make a man take in a stranger like Silas.

Is March. Snow Crust Moon. We sit round the table. Cold, icy winds clinging on to winter's tail and we doing our best to keep warm. Me, Lyle, and Hetty, bunch up, shoulder to shoulder under the lamp, help mama with the quilt she making. Above us, rafters hang with turtle shell, sweetgrass, axe, hook, all belonging to daddy. Wood smoke. Twins asleep. Boat roll and tip and the wind sneak in every crack so the stove got no chance of keeping up. It crackle through the yellow newspaper mama paste on the walls. Door open and it howl. There daddy and there a man next to him. A stranger, dark face in the shadows. He step into the light, handsome as a blackbird. But he all hunger and bone.

Daddy lean the door shut hard. 'This is Silas,' he say, 'Silas Moretti, he will be staying here with us a while. Some of that stew, now.' He look at mama and she get up and fetch a plate and motion Silas to sit at the table. Mama put a plate of stew in front of him and he shovel it up. He hungry as a bear at first thaw.

'Out of the prairie,' says daddy, 'got no home, nothing left after the dust and all. Got nothing.' He look at mama. Her face say, how we gonna feed another mouth? Find a place for a grown man to sleep? But she silent. When he finish Hetty jump up and take his plate. She all smiles. I see him look at her, watch her back while she walk.

He got manners. He say, 'Thank you, mam. That was the best stew I had in some long time.' He smile. Mamma smile. Hetty smile. Lyle turn away.

Then Silas look from daddy to mama and say, 'I hope you folks won't mind if I take some time now to study my bible. I do not like to let the day pass without some reading of it.'

Mama nod, daddy nod like he someone who read the bible every night and he even move the kerosene lamp near to Silas. Silas take his bible from inside his coat. It ain't as big as daddy's bible. Is worn, pages curl and damp. He open it and read in silence. We all silent then. Only the wind speak.

Silas sleep in the kitchen on the boards. Next morning he there at the table drinking coffee with daddy. Mama tell me go out and see if the chickens laid. Outside the wind gone west but it cold enough to freeze and the deck slip under my foot. On the bank the grass crackle frost. I am in the chicken coop, hand in the nesting box, pull out the straw-warm eggs. Put them in my coat pocket and look up Creek for December, look for smoke coming out the boat-chimney where he live with Hannah but there ain't no smoke, so I take the eggs inside and mamma fry them up for daddy and Silas.

Hetty up and she say she ain't going to school. She staying at home to help mama. When she ever do that before? She say it pointless going to school now anyways, she already sixteen and she be leaving any day soon, so why bother. I think of all the reasons why bother, why it ain't pointless, why it be the thing I want most in the world, not counting December. I think how I turn sixteen before long and surely I gotta be reading by then. I think all these things but I don't say. Instead I go

33

off out to the woods looking for the branches that fall in the night wind. Lyle chase after me, say he gonna help. Look like he ain't going to school either.

We collect the wood, chop and stack. Then Lyle go inside and come back with two tin mugs of coffee. We sit on the log that resting by the chicken coop.

'Daddy be sleeping and Silas too. They mighty tired if you ask me,' say Lyle. 'Like to know just what it is they've been up to. I reckon it's no good. Don't like the look of that stranger none.'

'Me neither. He look old and cruel to me. Way his mouth turn down and his tongue flick out and curl up his lip like the rattlesnake. But he gotta be a man of learning else why he read the bible? He like a preacher, only he ain't.'

'He too bad to be a preacher, no preacher look like that.'

'How come you know, and how come if Silas that bad daddy take him in?'

Lyle say, 'He just is and he got something on daddy. They got something they hiding. Ain't what they seem.'

'Like what? What they hiding?' Lyle just shrug. 'Well, how come you say that?'

'Just do,' say Lyle and he run his fingers through Castor's grizzly hair.

'That ain't no answer, Lyle.'

'Hell, don't expect none from me. Time you grew up, girl, time you see not everyone like us.'

'What is it you know that I don't?'

'All I know,' say Lyle and he pick up his hunting gun, put it across his knee and rub its barrel clean with that old, oily rag of his, 'is that banker from Lafayette, the one daddy took fishing, he ain't here and he's supposed to be, supposed to be coming back this way with daddy to pick up a truck. So where's he gone? And why is daddy talking about buying a new boat off Pike and a new motor and all?'

'So?'

'So, where's the money coming from? Ain't from taking fishing trips alone, and what does Silas know? When else did daddy bring a body home, another mouth to feed, someone he don't even like?'

'But he do like Silas.' Castor at my feet, nosing at my old boots.

'No he don't. He just scared of him, that's what daddy is.'

River swell in the thaw. Folk say there be floods. They afraid it be like before, when I be ten or thereabouts, when the river run backwards. Floodwater have nowhere to go then and it stay on the land all through spring and summer and into the fall. That year daddy and Lyle spend all their time keeping the boat tied and safe, doing repairs. Hetty and me using the buckets to bail out. Dead animals floating by, legs in the air, trees with roots to the sky, mosquitoes swarming. There be no school that year, no nothing.

But folks is wrong. The river hold its bank. Ice still lie in the cold places where the sun don't get and Grandma off chasing a flock of wild turkey that leave their tracks in the snow. I look for spring. Look for the birds coming back, the crackle and call, air full of wild cherry and plum blossom. I see it coming in the small things, a blade of grass that make its way up through fall leaves. White star of bloodroot, henbit and deadnettle, the first violet. Days growing longer, winter on its way. Is a good thing. I rise early to sun on the water, go fishing with Lyle.

Lyle say daddy getting to be a changed man. I say how can it be possible? He say, 'Surely you've noticed, Aiyana. When was the last time you seen him take off his belt to any of us?'

Is true what Lyle say. Daddy gone quiet. He still off fishing and the like but he take Silas with him now. They go drinking together too, at the outlaw, Elmer Glass's moonshine shack. Come staggering back, and if Hetty ain't up, which mostly she be seeing as to how she's taken to staying up late, they chase mama out of bed to cook up some supper.

'I notice,' I say. 'Is true, like daddy be walking on glass and he ain't wearing no shoes. According to grandma he like a cat on a hot bake-stone. She say Floyd Weir ain't himself, he be dancing to somebody else's tune.'

'Well now, while daddy's eye off the ball and spring's on its way, I'm cooking up a plan for us leaving. It gotta be soon, Aiyana. Last night I dreamed that daddy hanged Castor from the skinning tree, his guts were spilling over.'

'But that be just a dream, Lyle. Most likely you be thinking about the lynching.'

'Maybe I was but who do you think was responsible for that? It was the Klan, Aiyana. And daddy's a part of it. You hear what he says about the nation *losing its values and morals*. About the *blacks* and the *night rides*. You think on that, Aiyana, how they hanged that boy and him just a year older than me. Dragged him from the jail, hanged him and cut him open and all because he was seen out with a white girl. Could have been December. You think on that.'

6

Hetty like the hummingbird with its ruby red throat, her tongue spilling out, licking at the air, sucking the sweet flower. She hover and flutter, preen her feathers, whenever Silas around. Make him corn pancakes in the morning, put fresh coffee on the stove. She stop going to the schoolhouse, say what she need learning for now, she a grown woman. Come the fall she start work in the button factory. She know all she need to know, Hetty say. Beside she can help mama this way. Only I don't see her helping mama, it be me that do that, always have been me. Hetty don't really help none. She mooning round, off on the riverbank. Go watch Silas. Is Goose Moon. April come and he doing up Rockwell's old boat.

Rockwell's boat like some old bathtub that sprung a leak. Got a rusty tin roof and it full of things no one got any use for anymore. It near on half-sunk but daddy help Silas bail it out and mend the timbers with fine, new cypress logs. Where they get them a mystery, but they come by night and dark, like most things on this river.

He doing it up good. All the rubbish piling up on the bank behind and there always someone looting through the heap: rubber tyres, bent wheels, messed up fishing nets, a stove look like it burned itself out, pans black as coal, empty cans, papers, boxes and beaten up wood full of nails.

He strip that whole boat out and he painting it too. He paint it the colour of grass because Hetty say she like that colour. Fine days she there helping him clean it up. She even sew curtains and make a cloth for the table. Grandma say she got it bad, she bitten hard. She say no good gonna come of it, Hetty be promised to Johnson and what gonna happen when Johnson find out what she up to. 'It is a good thing that your daddy is busy with his fishing trips, too busy to notice. Though it will only be a matter of time,' grandma say. 'Floyd Weir wasn't born on crazy creek.'

There ain't no more alphabet now. Hetty got other things on her mind and she quiet as a cotton mouse when it comes to night time. She sad and she thinking. I not sure about what, sometime I think it Silas, sometimes I think it be daddy, especially when she cry out in her sleep. I ask her if there be something troubling her but she tell me, 'Don't disturb me now, Aiyana, just leave me be.'

I tell December about the alphabet and he say he show me from *M*. But he busy just now and besides my paper gone missing. I look everywhere for it but it ain't where I hide it under the bed. Someone take it. I reckon it be the twins as they always be up to some kind of mischief. I ask them when I get them alone, no one listening, but they deny it, say no, they never seen it, don't know what I am talking about.

I gotta get myself some paper and I gotta get myself that orange school book that Hetty keep saying she gonna throw away. Is an old reading book, one of the first she have. She say she don't know why she keep it. It be no good, she way past that kind of reading. But when I ask her can I have it, she say maybe she gonna keep it anyway, maybe it come in for when she got children and they gonna learn. I know where I find some paper. It be on Silas's rubbish heap. It got rain and river damp but it paper all the same. I see the black crow sitting on a whole heap of it just the other day.

Hetty there. Even though spring still cold as the mountain choked with snow she be wearing her blue cotton Sunday dress with the lace collar. She sitting on the bank under the willow, got her knees hunched up and her arms round them. She like butter wouldn't melt. Got red lipstick on too. Silas on the riverbank sawing wood. He stop. I wait. I standing in the shadows where they don't see me. They only got eyes for each other. He walk over to where Hetty sit and he crouch down beside her. He reach out his hand and touch her cheek. She looking down like she shy or something, he looking round like he wondering if there be anyone can see. Next thing they kissing. Next thing they lying on the bank. Turkey vultures fly overhead. Startle. They sit up, smooth their clothes. Hetty jump up then and she start coming my way. I take off like a whitetail, away from the river, under the trees.

Later I tell December what I see. We sitting in the cane chairs on Hannah's deck. There ain't much room what with the wood for the stove and the water barrel, December's fishing things, washing lines and rope, axes and brushes, pails and the like, all got to find a place somewhere. That be river life for you.

He back from the Ice House and he tired. His back ache and he lean forward so I rub it for him. He say that be nice and when we together we gonna lie on our bed and he rub my back too. I say grandma making us a dreamcatcher so nothing bad gonna ever happen and I fixing to learn to read and get myself a job so we gonna have some money to buy things, like a radio, maybe even a gramophone, like linen sheets and a turkey at Thanksgiving. Maybe we even think of leaving one day, go and see the world, travel on down to the Delta.

Ever since Pike Dummond show me and December that old map he keep in his truck and he trace the river with his fingers so we see where it go, a seed grow in my mind, one day I gonna follow that river line. It ain't that I want to leave now. I know what Lyle be planning but I hoping still we don't have to go. But river be my life and one day I need to see where it go. I thinking one day when I got a husband and children of my own we take that trip out of here where the land stretch wide, no trees, no river holding it all in. I think maybe we just float on the wind like the eagle, way down to the Delta. Reckon that where the river be most peaceable, where it stop troubling and come to know itself best.

December tell me he think it best say nothing about Hetty and Silas, is their business and we don't want to rouse up Johnson's wrath. He already an angry man, December say. He angry enough for two men. I know what he mean but I got my reading and learning to think of. I need that book belong to Hetty and I need to be getting past M.

We lying in bed. Hetty got her back to me. Lyle and the twins asleep. Owl wooing the night outside, flicker of light through the curtain now winter running away.

'I know what you up to,' I whisper.

'What?' Say Hetty.

'I know about you and Silas. I see you on the riverbank. I see you kissing.'

Hetty turn to face me. I don't see but I tell she troubled. 'Hush now. No you ain't. You ain't seen nothing.'

'Sure did. Only won't be fixing to say, not if you give me that orange book that you keep holding onto. Alphabet too. You teach me what coming after M and I don't say nothing to Johnson, I don't say nothing to no one.'

Hetty lie still. She thinking. She pull back the covers and get out of bed. She fetch the book from the drawer where she be keeping the things she saving for when she set up house with Johnson, like the linen tablecloth, the four china plates Ada give her, a quilt she make with mama from flour sacks, stockings and a nightgown and such. She get back into bed and put the book in my hand. I slide it between my fingers. Is silky smooth. I don't see it but I know it be orange and it got a boy and a girl that someone draw on the cover. I smiling in the dark. This my first book. My heart warm as a new laid chicken egg. I gonna learn what come after M. Hetty gonna

40

teach me. It be a secret. She got a secret and I got a secret and we gonna keep our secrets.

It be a fine spring day when daddy come home. Sun out, light up the river, water like a turtle back with it line and cracks. Teal and goldeneye got their chicks swimming behind, up Creek, making feathers in the water. This the time of young things when they gonna learn all they need to know for life. Time I never had but I sure am gonna give my young.

Daddy be home long enough to take off his boots and get him a plate of biscuits and gravy when a boat pull up outside. I washing dishes, mama lying down. Hetty be out on account of her not wanting daddy to know she ain't going to the schoolhouse no more. The motor cut, footsteps on the gangplank. Door open, is Johnson, standing there, shoulders big as the frame. He leaning into it and he ain't looking happy. He looking like he got something on his mind.

He nod hello to daddy. 'Hetty here?' He ask and he step inside.

'She at school,' say daddy.

'Is that a fact? That ain't what I been hearing,' say Johnson, 'what I hear she don't have nothing to do with school no more.'

'First I hear,' say daddy. 'This so, Aiyana?' He look across at me.

I turn from washing the dishes. 'Far as I know she be at school.' I turn back to the dishes.

'News to me,' say Johnson, 'more than likely she with that Silas fella you done bring here. He fixing up Rockwell's old boat and she helping him, that's what I hear.'

'She ain't helping no one, not if I got any say in it.' Daddy get up. I hear the thunder in his voice. 'Go fetch your sister,' he say to me.

I know better than defy daddy. Dry my hands on the cloth and fetch my boots and put them on. I am by the door, on the

41

deck when I hear Johnson say, 'Reckon you won't need reminding as to our agreement, Floyd. Am I correct?'

'Sure thing,' say daddy. 'Hetty yours. There got to be some mistake. You just leave it to me, Johnson. You can be sure I'll make it right. Come back tonight and Hetty be waiting for you. Time now you was fixing a wedding date.'

I hear the planks creak under daddy's feet. I am gone.

Daddy all storm and rage but not with me and not with Silas. Only Hetty. He take her outside and he beat her hard with his belt. This time she say nothing, don't stand up to him. He bring his belt down again and again on her back and she cry out in pain. Silas, he just sit on the log by the coop, head in his hands. Like a coward in his silence. I know what she done ain't right but she don't deserve the belt, least not like this and I ain't listening to her cry out like she doing.

Mama come outside, try her best to persuade daddy to stop but he ain't listening. It look like it up to me so I shout, 'Daddy that enough! She ain't gonna do it no more, leave her be. I'm begging you.' But he take no notice, like he in a dark world all his own. His face all red and puffed up, spit at the corner of his mouth. Hetty crouch on the ground, like a hedgehog rolling itself up in a ball. Lyle come to see what the fuss be. He stand watching, Castor growling all the while. Lyle's knuckles white from holding back the dog. Thin lines of blood seeping through Hetty's blue cotton dress.

Hetty go back to school and we go back to doing what we supposed. We forget about the alphabet past *M*. I get ointment from grandma to put on Hetty's back at night, help heal the welts. She cry and cry. Ain't no healing some things.

7

He don't look much like a cat, daddy too big for that, but he play like a cat. Is a cruel taunting, mostly he save for me when I be small, now I grown he don't bother so much. I old enough to see past the cat's leavings, past the dead mice, got maggots and all, past the broken winged blackbird, past the chiggers and ticks he leave in my coat. So when he tell me go fetch the nets he leave on the bank by the Bluff, I ain't expecting it.

I be afraid of the rattler. Bite, then eat, head first, swallow lizard, mice, ground squirrel, swallow a rabbit. Girl Hetty know, bit once and she sick forever. Rattler like some people, there be no warning before they strike. Dust from a rattler can blind a man, they say. Rattler kill a dog.

I looking across the water. Pike, our white-haired neighbour, be fishing there. Put my hand up to say hello. Step into the boat. The rattler rear up, red mouth stretch open, white fangs hissing, tail rattling. I scream out. It come at me, bite down on my foot. I scream, 'Rattler.' Then fall back in the boat. Wait for the pain to strike. Hear Pike splash in the water. Hear mama shout my name, come running to the bank.

'Gotta get her to the hospital,' Pike shout. He coming up out of the boat. 'I'll get the truck.'

Rattler move away, slither up the boat side and slink off into the water. Mama looking down on me. She drag the boat up the bank and pull me out. She shouting for Lyle. Pike shouting for Ada. My lungs closing down. Everything turn to black.

When I wake, look up, see the tin on the roof. Mama there beside me. Lyle and the twins. Pike and Ada too. They all looking like angels. Wonder if I be alive or dead.

Lyle got something in his hand, he hold it up to show me. Is a boot. Be granddaddy's boot. 'Look. Granddaddy's old leather boot, it saved you, Aiyana,' he say and he bring it close and show me the mark of the rattler's fangs. 'Good job you was wearing them, girl.'

'Good job indeed,' says Pike.

Ada smile and nod.

Mama smile and say. 'Good job it just be your lungs and Doctor Miller was up visiting in the Creek. He give you your injection. Just rest awhile now and you be fine.' She stand over me, smooth my hair. I fall back into sleep and dream of a river bursting with snakes.

'I know he put it there. Deliberate. Ain't sun enough yet to coax the snake. He been digging in the rattler pit. He get it especially for me.'

Lyle and me sitting on the back deck. Two days gone since the rattler bite my boot. He whittling a stick with his knife. Home early from work. Lyle done left school a week ago. He be working down on the dock, below the Ice House, packing fish. His teacher Miss Askew say he clever enough for a boy's scholarship but daddy say better he be a man with a job than a boy at school.

'It was him alright. He put the rattler in the boat and he knew exactly what he was doing. He wanted to hurt you bad, Aiyana. He don't care if you die and that's a fact. He do his best to hurt you, worse than any of us but he hurt us all and he lay everything to waste,' say Lyle and he bring the knife down hard on the stick. Lyle got a beaten look about him. He never admit it but Lyle like school. I know he do. He clever and that be a gift no man want to give away. 'Always saying how the frog does not drink up the pond in which it lives. Time he took his own advice and stop hauling in the fish like he do, just to keep the rich men happy. River ain't for their sport.' Lyle kick the wood shavings off his boots.

'Reckon you be right. Come messing up the water in their boats what with the engines and the oil and the noise. It frighten the pintails and the goldeneyes right out the nests.'

'Daddy beating and using the river, just like he beat and use Hetty. Killing it all just like he tried to kill you. Soon all the fish'll be gone because they're hauling up all the river treasure and daddy is just helping them. All he want is to make a quick buck. He don't care for no one but himself.'

I say, 'Truth be we in need of a buck. Twins need shoes, chickens need feed, always someone need something.'

'I don't care how poor we are, it's wrong. He ain't got a heart. I swear the only one he ever care about is himself and the only thing he care about is money,' say Lyle. 'Rich bankers don't know nothing but daddy he should know better. He knows what the river means to us, how it all works, nature and all. He is a killer and a coward that's what he is.'

'If you feel like that about the river, then how come you fixing to leave?'

'I don't intend beating my children, using them, selling my soul. I won't be like him, no sir. I got another life coming my way.'

'Nothing stop you living that life here on the river, get your own boat. Least there work here, not like the land where it all dried up. There precious little work out there, else why folks like Silas end up here on the river. Out there ain't nothing but poor folk and empty bellies.'

'And what do you think we are then? You think we ain't poor? Jesus, Aiyana, you can't even read and write, that's how poor we are.'

45

He hurt me when he say that. I am silent. Look at the river for an answer. Nothing come but the water begin to rise in my lungs.

'We don't even have the money to buy you the medicine you need.' Lyle lean back in the cane chair and poke the deck boards with his stick. Castor growl.

I breathing heavy, my lungs filling up. 'Ain't true,' I say.

'True as the day,' say Lyle, 'and if he didn't drink it all away and if he didn't take whatever he want, like Hetty. You gotta be careful Aiyana,' he say 'before you know it, it won't be the rattler, it'll be him, wanting what no man should ever want from his daughter.' He slam the stick into the boards. Castor bark. I see the red anger rising in Lyle's cheeks. My chest go tight, whistling like a woodchuck. Lyle stand up and throw the stick into the river. Then he turn to me and see how I be struggling for my breath. 'Hey, it's OK,' he say. 'It's OK.'

'It ain't OK,' I say, it come out in a long whisper. Feel the water rising up in my throat, fish taking my breath. River in my blood.

Back in bed. Water drip drop off the tin roof. Roof ripple above me. Is wet. It drip drop. Drip drop in the heat, drip drop in the cold, no matter what weather, even when the sun out, it drip dropping. I watch every night of my life. I think it watch me, watch Hetty, it know why daddy come. I look up. It all in a zig-zag, all crumple up. Look like writing on the page but what written there, what it say, I don't know. There be a word for it though and I know that word, it *corrugate*, that what crumple up tin is. I watch the tin, hoping it won't see daddy come. I think about what Lyle say and how it break my heart if he go and I don't go with him. How if he do my heart crumple like the tin roof. But he sound sure. Reckon there ain't no changing his mind.

If I know the word and the writing of it, I make a list of all the good the river do for us, how we got catfish and bream, turtle and gar, seine nets bursting with silvery fish, fat mussels, duck and goose. How if it weren't for the river we never see the snow goose walk on ice, or hear the whistling duck. I give Lyle the list of all the things but still I reckon he go. It ain't the river making his heart sore.

8

Summer come, is the month of June. Moon like a strawberry. Life grow easy and open. Our life outdoors now. Now there be picnics and fish fry and the mussels be boiled and scraped and the pearls dug out the shells. Everyone talking to his neighbour, though we only be talking to Ada and Pike. River folk drinking lemonade and beer in the shade of the cottonwoods and willows. Sun lick the morning awake, lick the trees. Leaves turn their backs to silver in the southern breeze. Sunlight spark on the wings of the kingfisher as it fly downstream. I am on the riverbank skinning squirrels with daddy when he tell me. I put down my knife. Stop skinning. I don't hear right, surely it ain't right. Then he say it again.

'You best make yourself ready, child. Soon as Silas finish that boat you are gonna live with him. You ain't a child any more. You're a grown woman now, old enough to leave. He be your man now.'

I pick up the knife again but I don't skin, I just look at him and I know he mean it. 'I ain't,' I say. 'I ain't.'

'You will do as I say, child.'

'No, it ain't right. Please.'

I hope he be softening up but I see his lips tight, his face set hard. He looking at the knife.

'No sense in you carrying on, pleading and the like. I already agreed. It's for the best.'

I stand up tall. 'I ain't,' I say. 'I ain't gonna live with him.

48

He an old fossil, like a piece of twisted wood, no sap, bent in the wind. I fifteen, sixteen soon and I old enough to make up my own mind and besides, December Lutz, he waiting for me.'

Daddy stop skinning but he hold on to his knife. He stand and face me, his hand shaking and he point the knife at me. 'I won't hear that name mentioned, do you hear me? Now, I'm gonna pretend you never said that because no child that go by the name of Weir ever gonna marry a coloured and that is a fact.' Blood drain from his face. I think surely he gonna pull me up and drag me to the water but he go back to skinning. 'What do you know anyway? Can't even read. Got lungs so full of water, the winter comes and you can hardly breathe, you're lucky to get a man like Silas and that's a fact.'

'But I don't want him. Is Hetty, she want him, she in love with him. He in love with her. He don't want me.'

'I already give you to him, child. Hetty's gonna marry Johnson and you are gonna live with Silas and let that be an end to it. As for December Lutz. He ain't even got a proper name, ain't even got a family to speak of.'

'He have, he got Hannah and she love him.'

'Hannah Lutz ain't nothing but a whore and a spy, like the old woman, her mother, should have been shot for treason, like all them square-heads. You stay away from her, you hear me. You stay away from him too. If I hear you been near him I swear I gonna...'

'I love him and I ain't living with that old crow.'

'Now that is downright disrespectful,' say Daddy. His hand move to the buckle of his trouser belt.

I am praying for the belt. The belt is not the drowning. Anything but that. I look him straight in the eye. 'I am learning to read,' I say even though it be a lie. 'I am gonna get my own life and I ain't belonging to any man.'

He undoing his belt now. His face gone red and his eyes big. He taking his belt off. 'Why, you asked for it, child.' He reach out, catch my neck, yank me to him and whip me across the back of my legs with his belt. My legs bare. Is leather and brass on flesh. He push me to the ground. Dust in my mouth. Bite my tongue so I stay silent. Screw up my eyes. Daddy swearing and shouting each time he bring down the belt. Might as well be falling into the water, choking, drowning. Belt and buckle open up my skin, feel like it reach down to the bone. Pain like I never felt before. Blood in the dust. I be going under. I be far away at the bottom of the river.

Hand shake my shoulder. Voice whisper in my ear. I open my eyes, slow. Lyle be standing there above me. 'Aiyana,' he touch my shoulder again. 'You OK?'

'OK.' I look up, his face boil with the rage.

Got welts like crushed berries now, but they healing slow. Go back and forth to Grandma, she dressing them with a poultice of mullein and clay. Give me black cherry tea, make me sleep, say, 'Sleep through this pain, Wild Plum, and no poison will come.' But I ain't sure poison already be running in my blood.

Hush fall on the boat. Daddy off doing river business. Lyle say he talking to the men from the government about the dams and like. Twins bring me paper. Hetty say when I feel up to it, we go on past *M*. I thank her but somehow it don't seem worth it. I am weary to my bones, like I am sick. My heart be as heavy as a mussel diver's helmet.

When Daddy come back from doing business, I hear mama tell him nothing change, he never change. He a godforsaken, wicked, evil man and one day he going to hell for what he do. He curse her but he don't beat her. Ask me, something in him know she can't take another beating, it kill her and that be a fact. I think I glad he beat me, not her. Time was daddy beat her hard. I seen it, but now it like a mist on the river, hard to see clear through, hard to know why she anger him so much.

One time after the twins be born, I see granddaddy come by and put a stop to it. He step right up to daddy, and put a

50

gun to his head. Tell him he ever beat mama again he gonna shoot him down. Least that's what Lyle say. I don't recall the words but Lyle do. He say daddy call mama a redskin lover and a squaw. Lyle remember everything and one day he fixing to pay daddy back. He don't say it but I know it for sure. I might not know the word but I know what live in people's heart. I know that. And mama's heart, it full of rain. Except for one thing. Only one thing make her smile.

She always have it, long as I remember, far back, she show me sometime when it just me and her and I sit on her knee. It hidden in the Angel Chest under the cotton petticoat she wear on her wedding day, in women's things, somewhere he ain't likely to go poking around like he do. I ain't remembering first time I see it but I know it look like me, might as well be me. She smiling, got her chin resting on the hands, they crossed, fingers wove together and her eyes bright as the first sun, like spring come and she real happy. Not like she mooning in love, not that kind of happy, just happy to be, the kind I feel when I be out on the river, only me and the water and the eagle.

Got a curl on her forehead, hair thick and dark like grandma's, shine like a new mirror when is washed in nettle water. First time she show me, she say, 'This is me, Aiyana, before, before I met Floyd, before I...' her voice trail away.

'How old you be?' I ask.

'Why, I was just fifteen, coming up sixteen, it was the summer before my birthday in the fall, practically the same age as you are now.'

'You happy then, smiling and all and pretty,' I say because mama be pretty though mostly she's forgotten how.

She smile then and smooth her fingers over the photograph, she get that faraway look, like she be floating off down river to another time and another place, right out of this life and I don't blame her none because ask me this life she got, it barely worth the living. She tell me then how she come by such a thing as a photograph. She tell me about the day the boat come.

'This boat was different,' she say, 'got a whole studio on board just for taking photographs, and a man and a woman taking them, photographing everything and everyone.' When mama tell me she excited as the day it happen, it like if she tell me enough, it gonna happen all over again, like she can turn back time.

'All the children, the little ones, came running that day. What did I know? I was helping grandma water the corn and pluck the crow feathers. They were shouting out about the boat come up from the Delta, with sails, two sails front and back, moored up by the Creek and they had a camera, like you put your head in with black drapes, a little dark room with a curtain pinned up at the back.

I couldn't go to see, of course, not right then because your grandma was listening and she didn't believe in photographs, said the camera steals your soul. So I bided my time, just getting on with cleaning the feathers, until the afternoon came and the heat and the insects were all humming and whistling and she fell asleep and I crept away then and down to the Creek. Saw the boat, sails down, resting on the mud bank. It belonged to the Gillards.

I took that gangplank past the geese and the children and I knocked on that side door. He came out, the Mister Gillard and he told me to come right in even though I said I got no money. He sat me down, told me lean on this ledge and he took my photograph right there and gave it to me. Said I was a natural beauty. I've kept it ever since, about all I got that is mine alone. And when I am gone it belongs to you, Aiyana. You are the only one who knows where I keep it. You are the only one, understand? And I'm sorry, I want you to know that.'

'Sorry for what mama?' She don't answer then, just get that faraway look again. So I nod because I understand. Everyone

52

got to have something belong to them and them alone, else how we gonna keep living when life so hard and dreams so few.

It be three weeks before I am out walking again, still my skin bunched and red. I am walking back from town with mama. Cross the railroad where trees meet, under the branches and leaves where it be cool. I tell mama I ain't living with Silas.

'Please mama. He too old and he got a cruel look. Grandma say he carry the thunder cloud with him. Besides, he like Hetty. I know because he always looking at her out the corner of his eye.'

Mama listen and nod her head. She say she speak to daddy but the way she say it I know she don't have no hope. Hope a thing she don't know. I ask her what daddy mean when he say Hannah Lutz a whore and a spy. She say it on account of the war that passed.

I say, 'Whore a bad woman, I know that much.'

Mama nod, 'Far as I know she ain't no whore, and she ain't no spy, nor was her mother. They were just from across the ocean, can't help where they come from, just trying to live a life like the rest of us river folk. If they are spies then so are we, what with our Ojibwe blood.' She sigh heavy when she say this and I don't ask for more. I see she sad as willow in the fall.

Mama not always like she be now. Time was I crawl up on her lap and she put her arms round me, stroke my hair, worry over my scratches and my mosquito bites, say she gonna get me shoes just as soon as daddy come home. Whisper how I be her favourite. I be special. Sing me the owl song, *Ku Ku*, like grandma sing to her when she small. A song for a quiet, sleeping child.

But those times long gone and I know, no matter what she say, daddy ain't listening. Time I be thinking what to do. Maybe I go with Lyle, he say he going soon. Reckon it have to happen, he stay and trouble follow like the track of the sledge in the snow. He still figuring when, but if I say I gotta leave now, before daddy give me away to Silas, he make it now. I know he be on my side. Go with Lyle and I be safe. But leaving the river, leaving mama and Hetty and the twins and grandma and December, it be too hard. Surely it ain't possible. The way it look, hurt come if I stay, hurt come if I go, ask me that ain't no choice at all.

I tell grandma I ain't gonna live with Silas. She say she already tried telling daddy but he ain't listening. He made up his mind that I'm for Silas and his will be a powerful thing.

'But I ain't his to give away. I ain't no man's. Woman belong to herself, ain't belonging to no man. I ain't his to give away, or do what he please with.'

'I know,' says grandma. 'You are Wild Plum and what he does is wrong but he is the rock that stands on the Bluff for all time that no man moves. And there may be more to this than we know or see. If I was you I would give serious thought to leaving with your brother, Lyle.'

'How come you know about that?'

'The spirits,' she say.

9

River still as a pond. Smell of fish and logs. Bugs swarming in the heat. Trees on the bank opposite, they upside down in the water. So the river be sky and the trees be water. I tell the river I ain't gonna live with Silas. I rather the river take me. It don't answer on account of it being so blue and so deep, where light don't go. I look down at the water-trees, down at the blue sky. I try to fathom its depth, see into the mirror of my future but I don't see nothing, only darkness.

Hetty barely talking to me. She find out daddy give me to Silas, that I be leaving soon as the boat be finished. I tell her I ain't happy. Silas ain't the man for me and I know how she feel about him. But she got Johnson too. I ask her how she love two men the same time but she say she don't and anyway it be none of my business. Then she go off moping and mama say it best to leave her alone. Mama say it happen sometime, it ain't always one man for one woman. Sometimes a stranger come along. I be sad for Hetty but it ain't like she being given away. Like she some piece of goods that don't belong. No, Hetty belong. But me, the only place I belong be the river.

Sit on the bank and press my finger deep in the gravel, sand under my fingernails. Trace my name, *A-I-Y-A-N-A*. Trace all its letters. Then I scrub it out and write the alphabet, big and small, as far as *M*. Only letter I know come after *M* is *Y*. *Y* be in my name. Not me, nor Hetty got the heart for learning right now. I say the sounds I know, send them skipping off over the water, like grandma's corn songs. It stop me thinking too much about what to come. It give me hope how everything be different when I know the word. I practice, over and over. Sit til the sky black and a swarm of stars come out. I praying I see a shooting star even though it not the season. I praying a piece of star break off and shoot over the far mountains then fade away like it do. My wish with it. But the stars they stay still.

Sunday and a whole month pass since I last seen December. Preacher Inman preaching at the Arbor and mama and Hetty and Lyle and the twins, they all on their way there. Silas gone too, he don't bother with me none. He no doubt hoping to get time with Hetty, except Johnson most likely be there. Everyone most likely be there except me and grandma. Grandma not for preachers and hymns. She got her own gospel, own songs, songs of the land, ain't nothing to do with the bible, she say. Grandma be our go-between, she tell December I hoping to see him and this be a good time. She tell him I gonna be waiting up on the Bluff, way out of sight.

Bald eagle spin over me, flying out the nest it make in the oak and the hickory, looking down on where the river curl away. I ain't waiting long before December climb up to me. He kneel down in the long grass and hold me close. Then I sit a while and watch him fish and wonder how I gonna tell him daddy give me to Silas. Is the only thing I been thinking of. Been thinking on it days and nights now.

When December see daddy's marks still left on my legs, he see red, say one day he gonna show daddy how that feel. I tell him it be my fault. I am disobedient. I ain't telling him the real reason for my beating. But if I ain't telling him about Silas then how he gonna help me and how we gonna be together? Just can't seem to find the words. I am like the boat in the whirlpool, turning every which way. Like the hunter in the snowstorm searching for the path, blinded and lost.

December take his shirt off, lay it out on the grass and make me sit on it. He kind like that, kindest man I know. Is blue, checked, soft cotton so the grass don't pain my legs.

He casting off. I watching his back, wide shoulders, like they got wider since he been at work in the Ice House. Thick arms. Skin like smoke. Sometimes December, his skin it black, sometimes is blue as a heron's back. He set the rod, then come and sit back beside me. I know I gotta tell him soon but I am afraid what he might do and say.

Ever since daddy tell me, I been afraid, afraid if it come true, afraid if it don't. My world look black as the eagle's wing when it fly across the sun. December put his arm around me and pull me close. He smell of apples and lye soap. I rest my head on his shoulder.

'What's bothering you?' He say. 'I sure as hell know something's up because you as quiet as can be, like the sun's gone out of your eyes, like when you don't get your breath and the river fills up your lungs.'

I don't say a thing.

'It's that beating, ain't it? Near as damn it beat the life out of you. I know he's your daddy but he's a bad man, Aiyana. Makes me about as nervous as a long-tailed cat in a room full of rocking chairs and it can't be denied. I swear he thinks the sun comes up just to hear him crow. Well there won't be no beatings when we're married. I been thinking though, might take a while. It's taking longer than I thought to save the money. Can't be rushing, Aiyana. Besides we got all the time in the world, if it wasn't for the beating, that is.'

'It ain't the beating,' I say.

'No? What is it then?'

'How many dollars you got saved?'

'Got fifty or more, but it ain't enough. You know that, so why are you asking now?'

'I'm thinking.' I lift my head from out his shoulder and look up at him. I stop, put my head back.

'What,' he say, 'what is it you're thinking?' His voice come soft in my hair and I feel his breath.

'I'm thinking maybe we gotta leave.'

'Leave?'

'Yes. Leave here. Start over.'

'Why? You crazy? What's there to leave for? Got everything we need right here on the river. Besides you always say you ain't never leaving the river. Never. So what's changed your mind? You want to be out there where they're all hungry and grubbing round for work, standing in the line at the soup kitchens. You want that? This ain't no time to be taking off... Hey, damn it! Oh Lordy! Got a bite,' he jump up. He straining on the rod, pull up a silvery blue catfish. It big. It struggle for life. I feel it. Is the way of river life but I hate to see that fish struggle. That fish be me. I know how it feel, mouth sorry, eyes sad and no breath. I won't see it happen.

'Lordy just look at the size of him,' say December as he reel it in.

'Put him back!'

'You crazy?'

'Put him back, December. Please, I begging you.' I clutch on his arm so he see I mean it.

'OK. OK. If it mean that much to you.' He take out the hook, pick up the fish with both hands and throw it back in the river. 'You sure are one lucky catfish,' he say. Then he turn to me. 'Reckon I deserve a kiss for that, don't I?'

Then we kissing, lie back in the grass, sun on our bodies, sure is hot, and I don't say nothing more. I just wishing it could be like this always. I ain't for spoiling it. I ain't for thinking of what to come. Lying here in his arms I am as safe as the blue catfish swimming under the Bluff.

10

Night fall and the Moon of the Horse rise. July. We glad of
the cool of evening now the days be hot and the air gone sour
like milk. Water down so low the mussels be jumping right out
the mud and the hogs feasting on them. Moths and lightening
bugs flutter about. Just me and Lyle and Castor on the riverbank.
Hetty in town with Johnson, mama and the twins sleeping.
Lyle make a fire. We toasting corn bread on sticks when we
hear them come, crashing through the trees. I know they had
too much to drink and I ain't waiting to see them rocking, full
of moonshine, so I leave Lyle and I hurry up the plank and go
inside to my bed. Lie there waiting for Hetty.

Hear them joking and laughing with Lyle. Loud voices in
the hot night. Daddy sound mighty pleased with himself, reckon
he be finer than a frog hair split four ways. Hear them talking
about money, about buying another boat and building a cabin
to rent to rich folk. Then it go quiet. Castor bark and Lyle
whistle like he about to go off hunting possum and raccoon
like he do. Voices fade. Air stop spinning. Boat creak.

I hear the footsteps, slow on the gangplank. Slow, up onto
the boat. They in the kitchen now. They coming my way. They
stop outside my door. Hold my breath. My door push open. I
know who it be standing there. I know who come. I tell by
the shape of his shadow. I pretend to be asleep, but it make
no difference, he still come in. He close the door and come
and stand by the bed. Pull off his boots, pull off his shirt,

unbuckle his belt and stand there over me. I am frozen. He draw back the quilt and I smell his moonshine breath. His hand come over my mouth then. He half in my bed when we hear it. Cry come from somewhere deep in the woods. A howling and there be no mistaking that howling. It be the voice of the lone wolf. Daddy take his hand away.

'Red wolf,' I whisper and he step back. He freeze right there in his tracks. He know the power of the wolf, he know the spirit of the wolf, how it be our protector, finder of paths. He know as well as I do red wolf be a rare thing in these parts now. He step back, bend over, pull his boots on. Then he grab my arm and he dragging me across the boards, up out the boat and onto the river bank. Moon take cover under the cloud. Ain't nobody but us and the howling wolf.

He standing in the dark water with me, my feet sinking in the mud. He force my head under. Hold it there. Then let me up like he do, so I gulping the air, then push me back down. I lose count of all the times my head go under and my lungs gasp fit to burst. I am falling away into the darkness through all the hidden stars.

First light from the east fall on my eyelids. I wake to the pale sky, my body half sunk in the mud, river at my feet. Hear the mockingbird rasp and trill and cry out to me. Then I remember the wolf. And I remember daddy. I gotta get away from the water but arms and legs, they ain't moving, they thick and heavy with river mud. My clothes and my hair too. It take all my strength to push up. I am like the crawling child. Crawl away from the riverbank. Crawl into the woods, find me the hickory hollow, fall in and lie down. I am the bird with broken wings. My soul gone left me, my being taken from me. Wonder if I am here at all, or if my spirit be the eagle looking down on its prey.

I try not to cry out. I think what grandma teach me. She always say, 'Remember, sometimes we go about pitying

60

ourselves, sometimes we think the world is a bad place and bad things happen but all the while we are being carried across the sky on beautiful clouds.' I look for the beautiful clouds only there ain't none. The sky be the colour of my wound. I close my eyes, drift into sleep a while, then the mist come up and I see my chance and I creep back and take the canoe and I row through the mist to grandma's yellow boat in the willow. I praying she ain't out in the woods yet and my prayers be answered when I hear her chant.

She singing from long ago, from forever. I wish I am that song. Right now I wish I be with my granddaddy. She outside dipping feathers, stop when she see me pull up. Ripple pool around me make the shape of my tears. 'You are early, Wild Plum, what is it?' Then when she see me close up she say, 'Look at you child, where has this mud come from? What has happened?'

I ain't saying the words, only climb from the boat. She put out her arms and I smell the sweetgrass and the morning corn. She help me up on to the deck. She half carry me inside and sit me down. She make tea, sweeten it with wild honey she keep in a jar. She bring water in a bowl, warm, and a soft cloth and she wipe the mud from me and then she take me outside and wash my hair like she do when I am small. When she finish we go back inside 'You ready to eat? Want some pancake?'

I nod. She put her hand on my head and let it rest there. Then she cook up the pancake and put honey on. When we finish eating she say, 'Now, are you ready to tell me, child?'

I am silent still.

'Someone has hurt you?'

I nod.

'Is it the stranger, the man who impersonates the crow?'

'No.'

'Another man then? Another crow has done something. It is Floyd, he has done this to you.'

I nod.

'He has forced your head under the water again. He has tried to drown you?'

I nod. Then I tell her about before the drowning, how he come by my bed and stand there breathing his moonshine breath, and how he take off his boots and belt and how he gonna climb in and how it only when he hear the wolf that he stop.

'I heard the wolf too, child. He is our brother. He knows what happens to us happens to him also. He speaks our language. He is our guide and protection.' She shake her head in an angry way, lips grow tight over the teeth fighting in her mouth. 'But if your granddaddy was here now. If he was here he would surely kill Floyd. See that gun, his hunting rifle, he would take it. He would fly across the water swift as a hawk. The hawk will kill the crow. He would spare him nothing, not even his skin.

Got a mind to take that gun myself, do the deed, only I am not sure that it works like it once did...' She stop then she look like she thinking deep. 'But I am no hawk.' She sigh. 'I am deeply sorry, my child. Here, come to me. Sit here by me. I have something I must tell you. It is time. It is time for you to know and I must be the one to tell you.' Her eyes fix on mine. She reach out, put her hand to my face and smooth my cheek like she do when I be just a child. She sigh like her heart be heavy with secrets.

'Floyd Weir is not your father, Wild Plum. Your father came with the railroad and left with the railroad and I believe he was a fine man. I believe his mother was Cherokee. That is all I know. I did not ask anymore. Asking is not always the wise way to an answer.'

She let me go, take her arms from me.

'I know,' I say.

'You know?'

'Well not so as anyone told me. Is just something that been

62

hanging in the air. Little things make me wonder and now you say that it all make sense. I know. Now I know why I don't belong.' My words come out calm but inside I am troubling. Is like my life be turned upside down. Now I know why Floyd want to hurt me like he do. I am another man's child, every time he see me, he see that man.

But there be more than this. There be the thing he do with Hetty, that he want to do with me. I sure this be a thing no man, father or no father, must ever do. It ain't right for a man to take a woman against her will, hunt her down, steal her spirit til it hanging like a trophy skin from his belt. Ask me it be a crime worse than killing. Be a living death that bring only sorrow and shame. I feel the tears come to fill the hollow at the back of my eyes. I fight them away and swallow hard.

'May the stars carry your sadness away,' grandma say and I see she be shaking. I look at her face, sorrow and fury all mix up. 'I should have known it would come to this, it was there for all to see. He will never forget you are another man's child. I cannot protect you. I am no longer strong like the wolf. My powers are waning. It will soon be my time. You must leave with your brother Lyle. Now. This cannot happen again. Promise me. Make me your promise, Wild Plum.'

'I promise.'

'Good. Now I will make you a dreamcatcher to hang at the door. To keep the crows away. It is about the only thing left that I can do.'

We sit outside and watch the morning come. I hear him. I hear daddy calling across the water for me. I wonder if he know I am alive. Then after him I hear Hetty and Lyle, but I don't answer. I ain't fixing on answering no matter how long, how loud they call.

Grandma sing *Ku Ku* while she loop the thread on the willow. She make the finest web I ever see. She give me milkweed to drink and sage juice, then she line my shoes with cedar leaves to make me strong and help me survive.

I tell her I must walk up river a while, let the cedar leaves do their work, find me some peace. She don't argue.

The trees be thick and dark on this side of the river, path ain't easy to find. Mostly I hide from the sun but when it catch me out and make it through the leaves, it fall green and paint me silver like the ghost fern. Times I am the ghost, I swear, no one see me, not even my spirit.

I find a place, take off my shoes, careful not to disturb the cedar leaves. I leave my dress on and walk into the river. Is cool first where the trees hang low but I swim out to where the sun fall like stars on the ripples. Is warm here and I float like an old turtle. I pray for the water to come around me and inside me and for him to leave. Let the sun and river wash him away. He ain't my daddy, he ain't even someone I know. Someone I know they never gonna do what he do. I wonder what my real daddy look like? Wonder if I ever get to know?

They all be wondering too, for sure. Wondering where I get to but I too far to hear the calling. Don't mind if they call all day long, night too. I ain't answering. Don't care who gonna fetch the water, wash the clothes, feed the chickens, help mend the nets. Maybe I never come home. Maybe I run away with December.

When I tire I come out of the water and make me a nest in the soft grass. Listen to the steamers coming up river, the calling of the loggers and fishermen. I sleep a while, then when the afternoon sun dipping, I make my way to where the ferry cross.

There a clearing where the road come down to meet the riverbank. Oss Starling, the ferryman, sit there on a boulder, chewing tobacco. When he see me, he say, 'Afternoon, Missy,' and he smile. He ain't got many teeth and those he got be brown with rot and he small and thin, got skin like bark.

I smile back at him. 'I need to cross over, only I ain't got no money. I might owe you, bring it back tomorrow, on my word.'

He laugh, 'On my word, well now, must be a serious thing.' He look across the river at the Ice House where it sit on the bank and the packing bay where the fish unload, where Lyle working, and where the boats dock. 'You be after meeting your brother when he come off shift, eh, or maybe your sweetheart?' He smile again and spit brown juice in the dust.

I nod.

'Climb aboard then,' he say, 'can't keep 'em waiting.'

The ferry just wide and long enough for one car, got a flat bottom with a trap door to shovel water out. Oss loose the line to the bank and pry the ferry away with the pole. He jump on. It move slantwise, like a sidewinder. I hold onto the railing and we glide, glide right across to the other side where the bank be concrete. Oss let me off.

'Bring the ten cents tomorrow, I swear,' I say.

'I won't be needing your ten cents,' say Oss. 'It's on the house. I was nigh on ready to cross anyways, always do when the shift finish. Hurry up now or you'll be missing him.'

I am on the road to the Ice House gate, thinking how Oss Starling be a good man even if he do look like a tree with things growing on it, and how come some men are good and kind and some are evil?

I wait at the Ice House gate, watch the men coming through. Hoping December see me and his eyes light up, hoping he put his arms around me and I gotta fight to hold back the tears. But when he see me it ain't like that. His eyes ain't got the light. He look like he puzzle when he see me. Not like he be glad. I think surely he be pining for me like I be pining for him, but it don't look so. Is more a, what-you-doing-here, kind of look that he give me.

'I got the row boat,' he say and I follow him along the bank to where it tied up away from the log chute and the packing and loading dock. He steady the boat for me to climb in and I think this be the time to tell him everything, now we out on the river alone together but before I speak he say, 'Lyle told me,' and he look different, like he all grown up. 'Lyle said your daddy is expecting you to go and live with Silas, said he near as damn it sold you.' He keep rowing and he don't look at me, like he be ashamed.

'Is true. Only he ain't my daddy.' I don't say more.

'Well it ain't right, Aiyana, it just ain't...' he stop speaking and look at me. I see he don't exactly know the words to say and it like he pretending to be angry when he not. Is like he ain't heard what I say. Like he give up hope already. 'As soon as I get the money we'll leave. I promise.'

I know then something ain't right because he don't say, 'We leaving now, Aiyana, tonight, no way you ever going back there, no matter about money, no matter.' This what he don't say. He just row and he look scared like a man out in the deep and can't swim. I seen that fear. I been that fear. I ain't wanting that fear for him.

'We find a way.' I say. 'Besides, Silas don't want me, truth is he want Hetty and I find a way to tell daddy that. I make it right see if I don't.' I ain't telling about what happen last night. How I gonna tell someone that? How you tell the man you gonna marry that?

December quiet, don't say nothing. I look at his face but I don't see no hope. Something change. Maybe he know it ain't no use defying daddy. Floyd Weir ain't a man to argue with, everybody on the river know that. He a man who take what he want, no matter what it cost.

Is late by the time I get home. Wishing I be some place else but what choice I got? Where I gonna go? They all out on the riverbank, all except mama, she inside finishing up the supper dishes. Daddy and Silas chopping wood. Is like they don't see me, keep turned away. Keep chopping. Backs to me. But then I see his shoulders shift and he turn his head and he see me. I know he see me. I am the ghost come back.

Hetty say, 'Sure have been worried about you, Aiyana. Lyle

66

been looking everywhere. Been to grandma's too. Where you been? You hungry? Sit here by me. I fetch you something.'

Lyle, he hand me a cup of orange soda. His jaw set hard and he looking across at daddy and Silas.

Hetty come back with some fried green tomatoes. 'Ada's best,' she say. But I don't feel like eating none. 'You OK?' She ask and she put her hand on mine.

Lyle sit next to me and he whisper so low I barely hear. 'Pack your things. We're leaving tonight. When they go looking for moonshine we're gone, Aiyana. You understand?'

I nod. I know it has to be. There ain't no other way.

11

Creep, out under the stars, song of the night frogs, moon and papery moths. Got me a bundle of things, tied up in an old knitted blanket: grandma's dreamcatcher, best Sunday frock, pair of shoes Hetty give me, cake of soap, my orange book, a piece of mama's cornbread and a wedge of cheese.

We be hiding under the trees, on the riverbank, Lyle and me. He tell Castor to hush up, tell me we gotta leave and there be no goodbyes. 'If we say goodbye, mama or grandma most likely gonna stop us.'

'OK,' I whisper, even though I know grandma think it best I go. 'Just one thing. I gotta tell December, I ain't leaving without telling him. I gotta go there first. Please, Lyle.'

'One quick goodbye and that's all?' Say Lyle.

I nod. 'Promise.'

'OK. But then we heading right off to the railroad fast as we can, understand?'

I nod.

'You sure?'

'Sure.'

Lyle set off to Hannah Lutz's boat, to where it moored up bank under the twisted willow. Castor follow. Me behind. Keep under the cover of trees, glad of summer, glad of leaf and cloud that hide the moon. When we get there, we stop and crouch down, Lyle whisper. 'OK, go now, quiet as you can, call him out, quickly now. I'll wait here in the bushes with Castor. Two minutes is all you got, girl. I mean it.'

I stand up, step silent as I can from bushes to riverbank path, come to the back of the boat by the gangplank. There smoke coming from the chimney. I hoping he be there, maybe even sitting outside, cooling off. I call his name, 'December, December,' soft and low, like when grandma sing. Nothing come back. I call again. Nothing.

I step on the plank, it creak under my feet. Tiptoe down, still whispering his name, knock on the door, quiet, gentle. I praying please God let him hear me. I thinking please God I won't have to leave and him not knowing where I am. I be standing there praying like this when I hear Lyle whistle out of the bushes and I know I gotta go. I turn away but as I do the door crash open. Arm fly out. Fist like an iron claw grab me and push me down on the deck. When I look up I see that fist, I know it. That fist belong to the man who ain't my daddy. It belong to Floyd Weir. And Hannah Lutz, she standing there right behind him and if I ain't mistaken they looking mighty close. They looking like a man and his sweetheart.

Floyd pull me up, put his hands to my neck, push his face close to mine, his eyes white as a fox's in the night, and he tell me I ain't never to be telling anyone I see him here and I ain't never to come looking for December again. He tell Hannah to go back inside and close the door. He take his hands from my neck, hold fast to my arm, nails digging in my flesh and he dragging me off the boat and up onto the bank. Only thing I grateful for he don't beat me none and he don't see Lyle waiting. Just see to it that I go home with him. All the while my spirit be sinking like the dawn moon but I glad he don't see Lyle and Castor. I hoping and praying they get away.

I sitting with mama out on the deck when Lyle come back with Castor. Look weary, come empty handed, must have hidden the bundles in the woods. Most likely he regretting having me along. I am sorry he be back but I am glad to my heart to see him. Don't know why he still hanging around waiting on me when he might be far away on the rails by now.

Days pass, weeks come and go and still Floyd watching every move I make. I tell Lyle, leave without me. Is for the best. But Lyle ain't gone yet. He say soon daddy forget about watching me, then we free to go. He say maybe we don't even have to go because we got something on daddy now. Something we seen with our own eyes, is just a matter of fixing how to use it. I tell him he got to be careful, Floyd ain't afraid of Lyle or what he know and that's a fact.

August come. Moon of the Chokecherry. Heat don't give up. Land suffering and the river low like it gotta a thirst forcing it underground. Is too hot to fish. Too hot for most anything. Hetty got a date fix for her wedding with Johnson though I ain't sure her heart be in it. Seem to me it happen awful sudden. She don't have much to do with Silas now and he out all day at the slaughterhouse where Floyd find him work. Nights he mope around, read his bible, don't speak to no one, not even Hetty. But he look at her and she look at him when they think no one around be watching.

Mama helping Hetty make a dress, they sitting by day in the shade under the cottonwoods and for once mama seem happy, she even sing when she sew. She making a veil too like they got in the catalogue.

Hetty tell me Silas's boat be finish before long. She hear Floyd tell Silas I be ready, and there be no need of a wedding for me and no need of a dress. Hetty say every girl gotta have a wedding and I gotta borrow her dress. But I ain't interested in fancy white cotton and lace, it be white paper I need, and pens and writing and books. I thirsting for them. One day gonna have me a table all to myself, full of books to read and books to write in, by a window where I see the river and the sky. I be reading everything then not just itty bitty words like *a* and *the* and I forget then there ever be such a time as this time.

School be out and the children all running in the rice fields, hanging down by the water. I ain't seen December, even though I be watching the river every night for him coming back from the Ice House. I thinking I go and see Pike, give him a message for December. So I ask Lyle to write a note that say I miss him and I need to see him, ask him to meet on the island. Lyle do it, though he say I gotta pray no one find out

Ada in the garden watering her tomatoes. She put down the can when she see me coming. 'Why, here's Aiyana come visiting.' She call over to Pike. Pike on the deck smoking. He take his pipe out his mouth and beckon me over. Ada say it hotter than a hog roast and she gonna fetch some lemonade.

Their boat blue. Fresh paint, got big pots of black-eyed Suzy growing up canes. I see Ada been watering them too. The pots wet and the deck wet too. Is cool on my feet.

'Now then, child, what can we do you for?' Say Pike.

'Got a message for December, was hoping you might take it. I been looking out for him rowing home from work but I ain't seen him. Maybe it due to the river being so low and all.'

Pike look at Ada. Ada look at Pike. Like they know something. 'Well now, it may be the river but I don't reckon so. Might be that he calls in on the Stamper boat on the way home. He been rowing that's for sure.'

'The Stamper boat? Henry Stamper's boat?' This be a puzzle to me.

'Reckon so,' say Pike.

Night come. Hetty lie next to me. I ask her if she be feeling nervous about marrying Johnson and all. She reach out for my hand in the dark. She say she glad she leaving, she gonna have a better life and maybe it ain't gonna be so bad for me with Silas, at least I be out of daddy's way. She fall asleep. I lie

71

awake, for once I ain't thinking of December or Floyd or going to live with Silas. I am thinking about Henry Stamper.

Henry Stamper only got one arm on account of logging. His arm got caught in the saw blade and that be the end of it. He don't log now, mostly he go out hunting and he sell meat, though he give Hannah meat free of charge. I been there when he deliver it, he kind like that. Maybe December gone to thank him. The Stamper boat be on the way back from the Ice House. It moor alone and it different from most others on account of Henry's wife Crystal. Call herself Crystal LaCott. She a singer once, that be her name then and she still go by it. Ask me, I don't blame her. Why she change her name just because she marry a man?

Stamper boat clean, white and fancy with railings and balcony. Is spilling over with plants and flowers, rosemary and pink geranium trailing down the sides. Is like Crystal, good looking. Like she be in her Sunday red shoes at the Arbor. See her there in my mind's eye. Remember how she brush the crumbs off December's shirt, flutter around him, happy as a tick on a fat dog. I paint that picture over in my mind and I see why December might be stopping off at the Stamper boat on his way home. It don't take a person of genius to work that out.

Next evening, night fall, I be waiting for December out on our island, hiding in the soft rush and switchgrass. I wait til the grasshoppers sleep. Wait til the sky turn to ink but he don't come.

12

Drought ain't broken though everyone praying and making offerings. It rain frogs but it don't rain rain. Crops withering on the stem. Grandma say is because the spirits ain't pleased, because man don't know how to look after what he be given, we forgetting the beauty and all. Land and life is a precious thing and we wasting it.

She ask me most every day why I still be here. I tell her we planning on going, soon as Hetty's wedding over. I don't tell her what happen, how we find Floyd and Hannah together. I think she don't need the troubling cause she ain't herself. She look weary, like she got the hunger, got bones sticking out. She don't hoe corn like she do and she don't sing to it no more. She ain't well, I tell just by looking, mama tell too. I ask her if she be OK and she say, time getting near for her to make her journey. She got a far away look, she had enough of life here. Say she ain't coming to the wedding. I say she gotta. She don't go, I don't go.

Is a fine, hot day, the day of Hetty and Johnson's wedding and I am up with the songbirds, out picking coneflower, bee balm and mallow for Hetty's bouquet. I put them to cooling and drinking in a bucket full of spring water, then row across the river blue as sky to fetch grandma.

Grandma got her hair in plaits. She dress in her fine, long robe with the fancy beadwork, hawk bells, shells, and thimbles sewn in. When I bring her across and she step up onto our boat leaning on my arm, Silas take one look at her and he don't hang around, say he going to the Arbor, help with the canopy. Ain't hard to see the sadness hanging over him. Anger too. Is mostly because of Hetty, I know. But he been carrying that black storm cloud since the night Floyd bring him home. God help me, it ain't a cloud I want to live under.

Before long, the men set off, Floyd, Lyle, the twins all in their Sunday best, leave grandma, mama, Hetty and me alone. I wishing it always like this, always peaceful. I wishing it be a world of women and I get to learning what I need to know and there ain't no beatings or fear. Only us.

Mama fussing over Hetty's dress. Is like a Sunday best frock but it mostly white, got a pale flowery pattern and a lace collar. She got red shoes too, like Crystal's. Hetty curling her hair while I fashion the bouquet, tie it with straw and white ribbon mama give me. Make it look real pretty.

Ada bring a big oval mirror for Hetty to see herself in. It ain't foxed. It clear as a river spring and we all stand behind Hetty, peering in. She smile then when she see herself, and our faces too, we all smile, even grandma smile. I wishing I had a camera. I take a picture in my mind. Hoping I remember it always. Hoping it be a happy day for Hetty. Maybe she get what she want at last.

Johnson promise Hetty a house on dry land. No river life for her once they married. Which ain't surprising because right from the time Hetty be small she say she ain't living on the river. Floyd reckon she an ungrateful child, what with the river giving us life and all, but Hetty say the river take life, it swallow you whole so you drowning alive. If the river don't kill you, then it make you sick with its damp and cold, gnawing at your bones, sucking at your blood like a worm under the skin. Is why she make Johnson promise to build her that house with a porch and a veranda and paint it white. She already sewed the lace curtains.

Riverbank thick with folk making for the Arbor, river folk and dry-landers, all walking to Sunday prayers and to Hetty and Johnson's wedding. We following them, do our best to keep the dust off Hetty's shoes. The Arbor be fresh and green, it got new leaves woven in with verbena and everyone crowding under it for shade. Soon as we get there grandma sit down on the front row, even though she don't like prayers. I go looking for December. Can't help myself. I waiting for my heart to know the shape of his shoulders so it leap up, but I don't see him. I see Floyd and Silas over by the picnic tables and Floyd give me that look he so fond of now, it say mind you keep your mouth shut, child.

I turn away and look for mama then I see she standing right next to Hannah Lutz and they smiling and talking. Hannah Lutz be standing there bold as brass, cold eyes and thin lips, gossiping with mama and I ain't the only one see it. Lyle here too, he next to me now and he look like he ready to do something rash, ready to put his hands on her neck and squeeze the life out of her, the way Floyd squeeze the life from mama. Then Hannah wave at us like we her lifelong, all time friends and mama turn and they come over to where we standing.

'Good morning, Aiyana,' say Hannah. 'Good morning, Lyle.'

I nod, don't speak, don't smile. Lyle, he mumble something.

'Fine day for it and your sister looking as pretty as a picture. Now, I think December is here somewhere. I'm sure he is. Saw him over by the picnic tables,' she turn. 'Yes, there he is,' she look at me and point and smile. Is the smile of the cat. She know exactly what I gonna see.

I turn and see them, Lyle see them too. December be standing by the tables, next to Crystal LaCott. She wearing her Sunday red shoes and she smiling and looking at him like a mooning calf, woman twice his age, and there ain't much room between them, not like there should be. They close as lovers, prettiest pair you could wish for. Hank Stamper ain't nowhere to be seen.

Lyle pull me away, say prayers starting up soon and we got to go find Hetty. When we far enough away from Hannah Lutz, he stop and he look hard at me and I got nowhere to hide.

'Don't cry, Aiyana,' he say. 'Don't cry. He ain't worth it. I swear.'

'I ain't,' I say. 'I ain't crying.' But my heart be like a falling stone and my lungs choking with tears and river water enough for a drowning.

13

September, Rice Moon. Mornings got the whisper of what to come, mist hanging over the river, sun rise to burn it away. Silas tell daddy the boat be ready. Daddy tell me to gather up my belongings. I am moving in with Silas. I tell Lyle we gotta go. He say he have the money by the weekend. Get us a ticket and we don't even have to jump the rails.

Hetty come home, help me pack my things in a cardboard box got from the Store. Put in the pillows mama give me that she wash in sage water, the bed sheets, the old quilt fraying at the edges, my dress, my winter boots and stockings, my coat and grandma's dreamcatcher. Hetty give me a comb and a mirror she been saving for me and a cake of lye.

I tell Hetty I can't go. 'If I been to school like you, high school and all, I be making my own way, not depending on what daddy say. Not belonging to any man.'

She say, 'Silas is a good man. You just gotta give him a chance.'

I say, 'You go live with him then.'

Hetty say, 'You know I can't do that. I'm married to Johnson, but if I weren't then maybe I would marry Silas.'

'He ain't marrying me Hetty. He just taking me. Besides, how do you know he be a good man?'

'I just do.'

'It ain't possible to know if someone be good when you ain't living alongside them every day.'

'But he's been living here with us since daddy found him.'

'He be a stranger, hardly speak a word. Besides river ain't in his blood. His blood all prairie and dust.'

'That is just nonsense,' say Hetty.

'I gotta take the book.' I go to the drawer and lift out the orange book. Is still where I put it, back under Hetty's old nightgown.

'You hid that? And all it is, is just some stupid old school book that's worth nothing.'

'It ain't stupid, is worth something. I can learn the word reading from this book just like you did. You can still teach me Hetty, or December, maybe he teach me.' Shiver run down my back as I say his name.

'But December ain't gonna help you. You can't go seeing December now Aiyana. Besides he...' She stop.

'Why not?'

'You know why, Aiyana. Daddy forbids it.'

I think about telling her how Floyd ain't my daddy but I ain't sure it will help none. So I just say, 'But December be my friend.'

'He is more than a friend.'

'He is not. We ain't done nothing, I swear, well hardly.'

'You're gonna live with Silas. He's your man now, Aiyana. Forget December. Besides his mind is elsewhere and you know it, he got a crush the size of a mountain on Crystal LaCott, and there ain't no moving mountains. You're lucky Silas wants you what with your lungs and all.'

I see there ain't no point in arguing with Hetty. I pick up the book, put it in my box under the clothes where nobody gonna find it.

When everything be packed and it growing dark and the birds settling down for the night and the twins be sleeping, I tell mama my breath come short, I gotta go out to catch me some air.

Mama look at me like she know what I be after but she

78

nod and say, 'Not long now, Aiyana. You be back before your daddy, mind.' She come over to me then and put her hands on my shoulders and kiss my forehead. She smell of sage and molasses. I think of telling her I know that Floyd ain't my daddy but I reckon it might cause her pain so I just put my arms around her. I ain't wanting to leave. I am wanting to stay on the boat that I grow up in with my mama.

Evening cooling. Leaves crackling under my feet. Trees come and go. Tree ghosts and spirits float on the water, wings whisper, swans' wings from the north. Soon the heat will die and the geese follow. Rice moon, falling leaves moon, songbird fly away moon. I am like the coyote. Too shy to show itself. Hear it howl in the distance.

Even though it be forbidden, I making my way to Hannah's boat. I hoping to see December one last time before I go live with Silas. When I get there, I stop, hold on to the willow that twist its arms around itself. The boat be in darkness, ain't no sign of her, ain't no sign of December. Even though I send a new message with Pike that morning. He ain't here. I think maybe his heart be full of ice like they say. Maybe a woods colt ain't never gonna be faithful on account of not truly knowing where he come from. Maybe that be the reason. I watch and wait but he don't show. The wind blow up, catch the falling leaves. I know it be time for me to go home before Floyd find I am missing.

I lie in my bed, boat rocking and me praying for a storm to come. Praying for a storm like the one that blew the old house of doors belonging to the Hartleys up by the very roots and clean across the pasture. Blew Pike's hen house away too, near blew off grandma's roof so it need patching good and proper. I pray for a storm to break up the fishing boats, and loose the logs, bring the trees floating downstream. I think a storm come like that and maybe Floyd get to thinking it a bad omen, maybe he change his mind after all. But no storm come, just the river running on, forever. Grandma say it like a nation's tears. But I say they my tears and there ain't no end to them.

Floyd give me to Silas like I be worth nothing. Like I got no soul. Like I just something nobody want. Silas say there only two things I gotta remember. One is a promise he make to me, there ain't gonna be any more beatings. I belong to him now not to my daddy. He say, 'I am not Floyd. I am not a man of violence, Aiyana.' I be grateful when he say this, but I ain't fool enough to think anybody save me from Floyd. Second thing he tell me, I gotta keep house and abide by his silence. Speak only if he speak. He say I do this and we get along just fine.

He tell me this the first night we be together, after he come home from work, after he wash and eat and we sit at the table with the lamp lit. Shadows falling on his face and on his hands that he twisting and cracking all ways. Like he got worry eating him up inside. After he tell me, he fetch his bible from the cottonwood chest, then he open it up and begin to read. I clear away, wash the dishes, make ready for the morning. After he finish reading, he say is time for bed. I praying God save me from this. I praying Silas go out for moonshine and leave me be. But my prayers like cotton in the wind.

He point at the bedroom and say, 'Go in there, take your clothes off and ready yourself for bed.'

I go in the bedroom and close the door. Sit on the bed, run my fingers over the ripples on the old quilt, think of me and December, how it be when we together, how it be when he take my clothes off. I hoping Silas have pity and be gentle on me. I bend down and pull off my shoes. The door open.

'Are you not undressed yet?' Silas come into the room and stand before me. He blot the last light from the window. I don't see grandma's dreamcatcher hanging there anymore. 'Why are you not ready for bed?' He say.

I am silent. Not thinking how to answer him. Not knowing

how to say I do not want this. I got another love. Another man I want to lie with. Silas step towards me. I see the window now, dreamcatcher twisting in the draughts and the last light falling on the boards. He close up, look at me but his eyes be some place else. Is like he look through me. Like he remembering long ago. 'Undress and go to sleep, Aiyana,' he say and he turn and walk away into the kitchen.

I sit and wait for him coming back. Watch the dreamcatcher that grandma make me, as it turn in the wind's breath at the window. She make it from honeysuckle vine she hang out to dry for six whole months and it got owl feathers on for protection. Grandma say every dreamcatcher different, take on its own shape when it weave and only good dreams come through the holes. But I ain't planning on seeing what dreams come through. I ain't thinking a dreamcatcher gonna save me, soul or body. Might be safe this night but there be many more nights to come. Who knows what happen? I be at the mercy of a stranger, God help me.

Light fade, I climb into bed, rest my head on the pillows mama give us, smell her sage water. I think of the sky above me. I rise up. I am the eagle far above the water, circling the Bluff. Listen for the river song calling me, is saying I cannot stay, I gotta go. I praying the night will pass. Make up my mind when morning come and Silas gone to work, I go find Lyle and tell him I gotta leave. Now. Lyle, he be my only hope.

Morning light at the window, dreamcatcher hang without breath and the river calm as an old swimming hole. Boat silent. I dress, creep into the kitchen. Silas be sleeping in the chair, head resting on his arms on the table. I put on my boots and go out to fetch water. When I come back he be awake but he don't speak to me, don't look at me. I make him coffee and grits and eggs, and he sit down and eat. When he finish I hand him a clean apron for work and he get ready to go to the slaughterhouse. He leave without saying a thing. Soon as he out of sight I leave too, back out hurrying on the path home.

When I get to the boat I call for mama. She open the shutter and put her head out of the window. 'Come in,' she say.

I stay still. 'Daddy there?' I whisper.

'He off fishing. Left first thing.'

'Lyle there?' I ask, 'he still in bed? Or he out working today?'

'Lyle? Lyle gone,' say mama. I tell she be surprised that I don't already know. 'He and your daddy got into a fight last night, Johnson had to come between them. Your daddy threatened to hang Castor, fetched a rope, made the noose and all, and hung it ready over the skinning tree. Lyle took off then with the dog, said he was gonna jump a train west and he was never coming back. I thought for sure he was calling on you to say goodbye. Guess he couldn't risk it. Your daddy says he ain't having nothing to do with him anymore, never wants to set eyes on him again. Says there ain't no place for him here.' Her voice trail away into tears.

I step on the gangplank, like I be walking in a dream, like my feet work on their own account and my head some place higher than the Bluff. I am watching Lyle jump, catch the rail and pull himself and Castor up onto the box car. Only me, I ain't with them when they be riding the rails out of here. I be left behind.

I comfort mama. We don't say much just drink some coffee and sit by the stove. There ain't nothing to say. Lyle gone and my hope gone with him.

14

Every day I steeping and scrubbing the pig blood and the cow blood. Smell of the slaughterhouse live in him. Live in me. Won't leave me be. Silas gotta have his clean apron. Apron gotta be white as a summer cloud. He inspect it the night before, ready for the morning and if he find a speck of anything he throw it back at me, and I wash it all over again. He got a temper too, when things don't go his way. Take it out on me, shouting and cursing, pick up a plate or such like and smash it or throw it across the table. Most times, after he lose his temper like this, he go off alone into the woods and when he come back he ask my forgiveness. He say, 'Forgive me. God forgive me for what I have come to.'

His habits be spotless and orderly, he always scrubbing his hands and fingers. Then he soak his nails in a tin cup with water and vinegar and dry them before he ask me to fetch his bible. Then he be as silent as a stone in the forest, as the river never be, as the fallen leaf be until you step on it. Is like he hiding something deep inside, like the fossil hide in the rock. First, I think it be Hetty, he missing not seeing her. Now I think it run deeper than that, it got something to do with how he read that bible of his day and night

He open it every night and even though I don't know the word I tell he ain't reading it. He just staring. He forget I be there watching, see him smooth the pages, see him pick it up, lift to his nose. He smell it and his eyes close and his head fall

83

back like all his longing be pressed in its pages. Bible be like the opening of a wound. I sense it, for I know what wounds be, know the smell and taste of sorrow and torment. Times I want to reach out to him but he forbid it. He forbid it in every way, shrink from the smallest touch, the smallest word. And he never look at me if he can help it. Keep his eyes away.

Nights he sleep in the kitchen still. He make up a bed on the boards and one day, when he off working, I go to mama and grandma and beg old quilts and pillows to make that bed so he can lie with comfort. When he come home and see what I do he nod and he say, 'Thank you.' He turn away then but I see his eyes wet and made of glass. Silas ain't used to kindness, of that I be sure.

'We can take turns.' I break the silence. 'I can sleep here some nights. Is hard for a working man to sleep on the boards.'

'Why?' He answer me. 'Why should you want to help me? I don't deserve your help. I have done much that is wrong. I have taken you as if you were nothing but goods for exchanging. I have treated you badly. Same as he does. I ask your forgiveness.'

'You never treat me as bad as he do. Ain't possible. He be the one to ask for forgiveness.'

But he be the one I never gonna forgive. I think a good deal about forgiveness. Is something I believe in, something I hear Preacher Inman talk about, something that live in my heart. But some things ain't for forgiving and the trouble be with Floyd he just do whatever he see fit, he ain't gonna change. There only so many times you take a stick to the dog before it bite you back. When hate grow in your heart it get too hard to keep calling forgiveness up.

'No, you ain't like him...' I begin, but he stop me.

'There is nothing more to say now. I remind you of the need for silence.' And we go back to living in his rule of silence, like our voices be lost and it the loneliest place I ever been.

I be alone as the wild rose in winter. Silas don't beat me with his hands or his belt, only beat me by not speaking but it be a cruel thing. Ask me silence be a powerful weapon that eat away your heart. Is hard to find the good in anything, blue sky might as well be grey, birds might as well be struck dumb.

When mama see me downcast she say she sorry it come to this. Floyd, he laugh and tell me to stop moping around. Times is hard, we all gotta count our blessings. We lucky to have the river keep us alive. Plenty of folk been turned off the land with the coming of machines, and the dust and more dust and no crops to speak of, everything rotten. He say we take what opportunity come our way and I lucky to have mine. He choose me a good man and it my duty to act a good wife. I best not think of running off like my brother because wherever I go he sure to find me. I believe him. He like granddaddy, best hunter this side of the line.

Grandma the only one who understand. She working on a spell to break this silence but she ain't perfected it yet, it gonna take a while. Now buffalo and black-tail deer gone, Indian ways gone too. No one care for the corn songs, and the things she need for spells be hard to find, hard to come by here in the South. She say meantime she give me some powder to make Silas itch like a skunk with fleas or a juice to make him sick like a dog. He sure to be hollering then. But what help that gonna be?

Wish Lyle be here to tell my troubles to. Wonder where he be. Reckon if I knew the word I'd be with him now, make my way out of here somehow. I think of December, always think of him. Wonder what he make of me living with Silas, and if he grown sick of his new love. I pining for the sight of him. I pray every night he will come.

October. Moon of the falling leaves. I am with Silas and Floyd and mama and the twins, we walking out of the Creek to the sorghum-making. Twins run on ahead, they busy poking at the turtles half sunk in the river mud, they got sticks and they prodding the grey shells. We tell them leave the poor turtle, he just getting sleepy, ready for the cold coming. We meet the others on the dirt road, horses, wagons, whole crowds of folk on the way to the flat field where the sorghum-making set up and when we get there it already in motion. Men be stripping the cane and cutting the seed head ready for grinding. Mule circling round and round juicing the cane. Juice heating up under the pine fire. Steaming and boiling. Sorghum gotta be cooked right else it go sour or be like sugar gone hard.

Mama help the women. Silas and Floyd help stoke the fire and strip the cane. I look through the crowds for Hetty, see her sat by the oak in the shade. I come past the children, turning the long rope, skipping in, skipping out. I thinking of Lyle and Hetty and me, and sorghum-making when we small, jumping the rope, our skipping songs. *Black Betty had a baby, bam a lam, li'l thing went crazy. Cookies, candy in the dish, how many pieces do you wish?* They be good and happy memories and I glad of them. When I reach Hetty I sit down on the grass next to her.

Hetty's baby show already and it barely three months since she married Johnson. I tell she proud of it, the way she stick it out and make it show. Johnson taking her west through the winter. He got some cousin working in a mine, gonna find him a job so he earn money to finish that house he building for her. Is a fine, dry-land house just like she want. Hetty ain't a river rat no more.

I been to visit twice now. Is near town, ain't far and it got a porch. Well, half a porch but he gonna finish it when they get back and she after a rocker and a table for iced drinks and she get it, no doubt. I gonna miss her, like I miss Lyle, seem like everyone leave except me. I tell her I wish she stay and I hoping she be back by the time the baby's due.

She say, 'Why, it won't be long and by the time spring come

I'll be back and you'll have your own bump by then.' She put her hand on her belly.

I don't tell her that ain't gonna happen, not the way it is with Silas and me.

'They'll be family,' she say, 'play together, just like the twins, up to no good.'

I too afraid to tell Hetty the truth. Just smile. Look back to where the men stripping cane. I am hoping he be here. But he don't appear, only Hannah there at the canning table. She look different, she staring out, looking nowhere. I see Floyd watching her. Is like he know she ain't happy. He put down his grub hoe, walk across. I see he thinking so many people, busy with the sorghum-making, no one notice. He right by her now and he nod like they just acquainted that be all, but her face light up like the fourth of July and he touch her back. I see it, a second and no longer, but he touch her. It is still going on, Floyd Weir and Hannah Lutz. It ain't ended. I feel bad for mama that he treat her like this. It be wrong and against God's teaching. But I think it be to my advantage if I make it so.

'Penny for them,' say Hetty.

'Nothing,' I say, 'just thinking about...'

'December? I see you looking. You gotta stop it, Aiyana.'

'I ain't,' I lie. 'I ain't looking for him.'

'Well, that be just as well,' say Hetty, 'because last I heard, a week gone, he got run right off the river and right out of town. Hear Henry Stamper was responsible, with the help of a friend or two. Had no choice according to Johnson. He knows. It's right too. It ain't proper for a man to be so fussing around another man's wife. A man and his wife is a sacred thing. December ain't coming back, not if he value his life.'

Hetty's words come like a fist at my face, knocking the breath right out of me. December gone. Run out of town. I try not to show my despair. Keep a hold of my breath and stop the drowning. I think hard on my breath and forbid it to leave. Stop the river in my blood from coming up and choking me. It ain't true. Can't be. But I look at Hetty and I see it be true and I already sensing my sweetheart gone and he ain't never coming back.

I think of all the things I might say but don't. Don't say he the man I love. Always. Don't care about Crystal, don't care for none of them. He still my love, the one who carry me when my lungs fail. He the one I grow up with. Never change. Don't say Hetty quick to see wrong, not so long ago she be meeting Silas behind Johnson's back. Don't tell her I know about her daddy and Hannah Lutz. I bite my lip. 'So be it.' I say. 'He figuring on going anyway. Best he gone and that a fact.'

Hetty get up. 'Probably is for the best what with his colour and all. You know how it is, Aiyana, the men round here they capable of taking serious exception to a man of colour, that's what Johnson says. It ain't right, a white woman and a coloured.' She brush down her dress, smooth her hands over her swollen belly. 'Now, it's time to eat,' she say. 'I got two to feed and no mistake.'

My breath come hard as we walk over to where the sorghum be boiling. The long table filling with dishes, covers off, picnics up, fried chicken, catfish, pork and greens, okra, fruit pies and pancakes, black apple cider, everything a person want laid out on that table but I ain't hungry. I leave them be. Leave them to the eating and drinking and the waiting to pour fresh molasses on the biscuits. Leave them to the harmonica and the wash tub, the fiddle and dancing.

I take my sorrow back to the Creek, slow steps, catching my breath, stop when I come to the willow. Sit under it, by his boat. Think of our days, of all the days we spend together. I smell him near, think on his smoky skin, colour of fresh molasses. He be my breath, my sky, now he gone my world be a waning moon. Who gonna be left? I ask the river. I listen for it answering me, listen for a song flowing in me. Bring him back, I cry, bring them all, bring Lyle too. Bring back my love. Is like the river don't hear, just go troubling on. Got its own way. Sometimes a river song just ain't what you been hoping for.

Yellow leaves weep from willow, fall in my lap. Gathering. Only thing I cling to is I cannot be here next fall. By next fall I be long gone. My mind be made up, ain't nothing gonna change it. I know now, for sure, what it is I gotta do.

15

November. Frost Moon still hang in the sky. First ice and water like broken glass. Look for him early mornings. Will he come? Listen for oars drop, slap at the river as he row down the Creek to the Ice House. Is a loosening in me. Like my mind drift. Like my eagle soar. I know he gone but I feel him close still. I am not ready to let go. Look for him in the evening, through the winter dark, rowing home, a shadow, nothing more. Long as I be on the river I look for him coming and going. December be the rhythm of my days. Silas don't seem to notice.

Now Hetty and Johnson left, Silas be in mourning. Don't say nothing, only necessities. Live in cold and silence. He read the bible, fetch it himself now, keep it in hiding, move it about. Never sure now where he keep it but I ain't looking. Find it easy enough if I want. Only so many hiding places on a river boat. He treat it like it the most precious thing a man ever owned and I reckon it be so. I reckon words be the most precious thing we might ever own, so one evening I gather up my courage to break silence and I tell him, 'I don't know the word, Silas, but I want to. Show me. Please?' He don't answer. Nothing come back. Is like he don't hear.

Ain't easy to say what be on his mind, what take him to roaming its distant mountains and plains, but it sure be a heavy load. There be Hetty gone, there be what Lyle say, that Floyd somehow scared of Silas, that they be sharing some bad secret, and me the price of his silence. But it be more than all of that, especially when he go off drowning his sorrows in moonshine and come back crying out in his sleep. I be sorry for him, truly, but every day he set off for work I think about leaving. Every night I scrub blood I think about leaving. Think about the coming of spring. By then I know the word. By spring I be reading and I be ready.

Ground under my feet frozen. Newspaper lining my boots but it don't keep out the cold. Cold stop everything, don't hardly see a soul on the riverbank, nor the river. Steamboats gone, fishing boats gone, only logging boats left. Wind from the east and the world grey as the mockingbird. According to mama, Floyd out trapping muskrat for meat.

Early morning, after Silas leave, I hurry. Finish chopping wood, go in, feed the stove, clean the kitchen. Take my orange book, wrap it in the paper I been saving, lock the door and step out. Grass frost-stiff, hands clutching so I don't drop it, is a precious thing. I am careful as can be, make my way along the bank to the twisted willow.

She be in. I tell straight away by the smoke from the chimney. I tiptoe down the gangplank, foot on the boat. Duck under the wash lines, hook lines, smoke fish. Planning to catch her unawares, her mouth open, like she just woke up and find a stranger standing in her kitchen.

Push open the door and there she be, Hannah Lutz, her back to me. 'Morning,' I say.

She turn, fast, look like she see a ghost, like the wind taken from her sail and she adrift. She take a step back. 'Aiyana,' she say. 'Aiyana?' Like it be a question, like she asking, 'What? Why? What you doing here?'

I silent. Hold my advantage. Put the book on the table.

'He's not here,' she say. 'They have run him out of town and if I'm not mistaken Silas knows something of this.'

'I ain't here for December.' His name hard to say and when

it come it still sweet on my tongue. Bring him tumbling back. Just like this very place. Call up all the times we sit here in Hannah's boat when she out working...

Winter and we got no school like the others. Just each other. Her boat warm. Different. Always. Maybe that be why Floyd like it so much. Ain't got newspaper on the walls like we do, got proper paper with roses and ivy climbing. Ain't got studs and rafters hung with tools and hooks, ice chisels, turtle shell and the like. Table scrubbed and neat set. Rocking chair and red cushion. It smell different, smell of spice, pine tree, smell of another country across the sea where she come from. Her mama and daddy's photograph be in a frame on the wall, looking down on us. Make me think of mama, of her picture which ain't got no frame, and she keep hidden away. One day I gonna get my photograph and it gonna be in a frame.

'If you are not here for December then why have you come?' Say Hannah.

'For this.' I do my best to steady my hands. My heart jumping. Pick up the orange book, take off the paper. I hold it up.

'I do not understand,' say Hannah.

'To learn the word,' I say. 'I gotta read books like this and you gonna teach me.'

She take the book from my hand and turn it over. 'This is a child's book.'

'Is a place to begin.'

'I cannot teach you.' She puts the book down.

'You must. I know you can. I know you teach December.' I wait til she look at me. 'If you don't, I tell mama. I tell the whole world about you and Floyd, about what I see that night. About what I see at the sorghum harvest. I know it still there, you and him. I see his hand on your back. I see your face. You don't teach me, then it be for the worst. Believe me.'

She wipe her hands on her apron, take it off, screw it up, like she got somewhere to go, like she in a hurry. She be the river fretting in the wind. I fretting too, trying not to show it.

92

Trying not to show my fear, for Hannah Lutz have a mighty temper.

I look across at the table with fine legs, small up against the boards. It got only one thing on it. The most precious thing she got. The gramophone. They bring it across the ocean, how they do that I ain't sure. Got a wooden box with a handle for winding and a horn that open up like a morning glory to let out the sound. She see me look and she remember, I know she do.

Me and December sitting at the table, no school for us and Hannah at work in the Store. Wind from the north and we trying to keep warm. We got coloured pencils and brown paper she get from the Store and we drawing. We quiet and that's how she like it. Everything fine and dandy if we quiet when she come in from work, her eyes change from grey to violet like the wood flowers. She as nice as pie. But her mood turn like a fish darting from the shallows, eyes black then, like she got anger deep in hiding. Floyd got it too, it come when he get the belt or the stick in his hand.

We tired of drawing and December he say he gonna teach me to dance. He go over to the table where the gramophone sit, take a record from the case underneath, shiny black with a red label. He put it on the gramophone and wind it up. Then put the arm across with the needle that made from diamond and the music start up, singing like it do on the radio and we dancing.

'Watch me,' say December, 'like this.' He stamping his feet heavy on the boards like he got wooden shoes on, throwing his arms about, pretending he play the horn. I copying. I stamping on the boards, boards like drums, pans rattle on the stove, boat shift on the cypress logs. 'We dancing on water,' he shout.

We join in the words. *I can't sleep at night, I can't eat a bite.* It the *Crazy Blues* and it make sense to me. When it finish he play it again, singing along, dancing so hard don't hear nothing but the music and our feet, don't hear the footsteps, don't hear Hannah Lutz come down the gangplank. Then there she be, standing in the door. She sure is crazy. Eyes black, she scream at him and me, 'Stop this at once. How dare you? How dare you touch my records?' She at the gramophone, take the needle off. Is like she don't see me, only December. She look at him. Pick up the broom hanging off the back of the door and she start to beat him. She beat him head to foot. She yell at me, 'Get out.'

I go but I worry for him. Crouch outside on the deck below the window, peep up and watch her. Is like she never gonna stop. He curled up on the floor and she still beating. Is like she someone else, like he ain't her woods colt child, like he nothing to her and never was. I know then, a beating from Hannah Lutz worse than any beating from Floyd Weir and that a fact.

She remember and she know I do too. But that be then and this be now and I ain't got no choice. Scared or not scared.

She look away from the gramophone. 'I cannot,' she say. 'If Floyd, if your father finds out, there is no way of knowing what he will do. To me or you. If he knows you are here now, he will be furious. You know this. I cannot do it. It is not my place.'

I pick up the book, wrap it in the paper. 'Well then, I mighty sorry,' I say, 'but I think I go tell mama what I know. You never see him again, you know that. And river folk take justice in their hands as they see fit, else why they run December out of town and it ain't just Silas do it, I be sure of that. They won't like you none, no, not one bit, for what you do with daddy.' I bluffing, hoping my fear don't show. I be scared Floyd find out, I be scared to my bones what he might do.

She sink down in the chair at the table, put her head in her hands. She look up. See her look at the photograph of her mama and her daddy, then she look at me. 'Alright,' she say. 'I will teach you. Mornings. When your father is not here. You only come when he is off fishing or hunting. We cannot take risks. You understand?' I nod. 'Not Wednesday, not Friday. I am working at the Store. We can begin next week.' She sigh.

'We begin now,' I say and I unwrap the book and sit down at Hannah Lutz's table.

16

Leave Hannah's, up on the gang plank, out on the riverbank. Make sure nobody see me. Hurry home. Back to feed the stove. Back before Silas. Look up at the white-snow sky above me. I am sky woman. My spirit soar. I am the eagle circling the Bluff. I know past *M*. Hannah write it down for me, on brown paper, she write all the letters. Got all the letters of the alphabet and all the sounds that go with them, like *S* for snake and Silas, like *R* for rat and river. When I be on my own I gonna practice them over and over. I forget some I know but she gonna teach me til I know every letter and every word. Now it begin, is a long way off still but it happen. By spring I know the word and I be ready.

Coming days, it be my secret, and I hug it to me. I think of telling mama but I don't on account of Hannah. Besides, mama got the sickness. River damp in her lungs, she cough and cough like she do every winter. I taking care of her, as soon as my chores finish I be there with her, make her coffee. Feed her grandma's medicines.

This morning she sit wrapped like grandma do in her winter blanket. Sit small, is like she shrunk. Like she growing old before her time. I wonder if she ever young then I remember the photo and say if she want I go and fetch it. She smile when she see herself, that girl back then. She cough but she smile. She sigh, say it like long ago but she be happy then, when she first meet daddy, even though her daddy make it hard, even though grandma want her to marry Ojibwe, even though she'd been thinking of leaving, of going to New York, thinking of new worlds, but she fall in love and nothing can stop her marrying, not even New York. Daddy different then, she say and the cloud shadow pass over her face. She tell me put the photo away, she say she got something else for me to look at, something from my brother and maybe we see him sooner than we think.

My heart leap like the hare. Sounds like Lyle planning on coming back. But right then, just as she about to go fetch what she got, boots thud on the deck. Is a sound we come to know, the hammer of Floyd's boots, it lie heavy as lead shot in our chest. He come in from trapping. Shake the cold off his back and make for the stove where he warming his hands. Give me a look black as a fish crow. Time I be gone.

I keep my hope that Lyle be coming back hidden from Silas. I am careful to keep my learning from him too, keep my eyes downcast. Practice the sounds and the words over and over when he ain't around and I ain't looking after mama. Practice them even when he be here, in my head, careful to keep my lips tight shut, keep my face straight as the gambler when he play the hand. Is my secret, the best secret anyone ever have.

Grandma the only one who tell I be keeping a secret. She know. See right through me. To her I am glass.

'Something is different, Wild Plum. What is it you are hiding, child? What is your secret?' She ask.

'Nothing.' I sitting in the rocker chair. She living inside her boat now on account of the cold. Animal skins hang on the door, smoke fish from the rafters. She wear her deerskin leggings and boots, wrap herself in the winter blanket. Cape of cedar bark hang on a peg, waiting for the rain. She at the stove thickening up the grits in milk.

'Nothing,' she say. 'Hmm.' She stirring the pan, window steam. She keep stirring, say nothing, then she take the pan off the stove and she look at me. 'Nothing?'

I nod.

'It's something,' she say. 'I know that it is something. I can tell by the cloud you carry, for once it is not grey, it is white with spring blossom. What is it? What are you hiding, Wild Plum? You have a lover? There is a man you meet when the stars crowd the sky?'

I laugh, 'No, no lover.'

'But you are in love. I see it written on your sky.'

She will wear me down, I know. Can have no secrets from her. So I tell her, 'I am learning to read. I am in love with words.'

'Huh. This is your secret?' She be disappointed, I can tell. Grandma like the idea of a lover. Maybe she dream of one for herself. 'Words huh. And this reading, who, who is it teaches you?'

'Hannah Lutz. But it be a secret.'

'Ah, the German woman, the adulteress. Your father's whore. You are blackmailing her then? No?'

I nod.

'Be careful, Wild Plum, she is a black day in summer, she is the thunder that splits the sky.'

I nod. I know this. But how can she know, how she know about Floyd and Hannah, that just a mystery to me.

'And if Floyd finds out…'

'He won't,' I say.

'And Silas, if he discovers what it is you are doing with Hannah Lutz, what will happen then?'

'I be careful. Besides, seem to me like he thinking of something else altogether. Is like he ain't belonging here. Hardly bother with me and that suit me just fine.'

'But if he finds out, then as sure as the sun comes up, he will tell Floyd.'

'Might be so, sometimes they thick together, they like brothers, going off to drink moonshine. Others he don't like Floyd one bit, I can tell. Silas ain't what he seem. One of these days I wake and likely he be gone. We both be needing to fly from Floyd Weir.'

She sigh, 'It was a dark day, Wild Plum, when your mother met Floyd. She was all for leaving until then. If only she had had brothers, if only I had borne more children, seen a son's black hair, felt his sleep breath on my face... You will leave soon?' She ask.

I nod. 'When I be ready, when spring come and I know the word least enough to get by. I leave then.'

'Until then be careful, my little one,' she say.

Silas

17

The child was perfect, slipping easily and wet into the desert of our lives, a rosebud mouth, eyes that were blue like her mother's, tiny fingers that grasped and curled around mine. She was as pink as a shell from the sea and her cry was healthy and strong. At night when Mary was sleeping I would listen out for the child, willing her to cry out in the dark so that I might go to her. Mary would stir and I would tell her, 'Rest, I'll go,' then I would lift the wet sheet from the crib and gather up the child, rock her in my arms and keep her from the dust.

Until the day of her birth I was afraid of nothing. I lived, a God-fearing man with a wife and a farm. I was raised there, worked the land all my life, carried on from my father when he died, saw my mother buried there in the scanty soil. I had three brothers but in time each of them gone out West for a better life, so there was just me and Mary to manage the land, the milk cow and the pigs. When the soil was lush and green, before the drought, we had a garden. But then bit by bit, year by year, the land around us turned to powder and ash and all our prayers for rain went unanswered. There was no rain, only wind. A fierce wind whipping up the topsoil, the fields shedding and the sky filled with the storm clouds of dust.

The day the child, Eloise, was born I felt fear like no day before it. I had a family now, we were no longer just two. I had responsibilities to feed and clothe and house and provide for my family, and do all the things a man must do for his kin.

It was something I'd wanted, I'd hoped for, but not like this. Not when our days were spent gathering dust, sweeping pools of it from the kitchen floor where it settled in ripples, digging out the fences, burying hungry animals.

Mary hung wet sheets at the doors and windows and over the crib. As much as we could, we kept the child indoors away from the heat and black clouds. We rubbed Vaseline on her nostrils and prayed she would not succumb to the dust pneumonia. We were a desert tribe, fighting a ceaseless battle and no end in sight, everyone praying for rain and the quacks like Thornton claiming they could blast rain right out of the sky with their explosives. But the way I saw it, no rain was coming, God had turned his back on us.

I heard it first in the relentless cough, that Mary had that summer. I knew it for certain when I came into the kitchen from milking the only cow we had left and saw Mary with her head bent over the sink spitting up a black clod, like an old man spitting tobacco juice. She was listless and breathless. It was as much as she could do to care for the child. Her milk dried up and we were forced to turn to cow's milk. Otto who owned the farm adjacent to ours helped us out with extra milk when he could and the child thrived as Mary ailed.

Dust seeped into every crack of the house, between every board and baffle, into every breath. I insisted that Mary wear a handkerchief tied to cover her nose and mouth. I began to think of leaving. Of taking Mary to a doctor, of abandoning the farm and moving west to California. We could pick oranges and grapes, we could surely have a better life than the one we were living now. I told her my thoughts but she was determined to stay.

'It will end,' she said. 'The Lord will provide, you'll see.' She insisted on walking the three miles there and back to church every Sunday, though there were times I had to hold her up. When she could walk there no longer, Otto and his wife Greta came for us with their horse and we helped Mary on and she sat astride it, carrying the child. The last Sunday was a day of celebration when the child was baptised. We came back to the kitchen with Otto and Greta, ate cured meats and drank a little of Greta's homemade beer.

On Monday the dust cloud rolled onto the horizon and the sky turned to night. By noon the chickens were roosting. By night I had buried my wife.

Otto found me in the kitchen. He laid his arm on mine. He spoke softly. When he came down from the bedroom, he told me, 'She is dead, Silas. You must bury her. I will help.' Then he called for Greta. Greta helped me dress her. I took her yellow cotton dress with the embroidered collar from the chest where it lay wrapped in muslin. It was the dress she wore on our wedding day. In death she looked as she had that day, a happy young bride and I wished I had a posy of wildflowers, like the one she carried, to bury her with. Otto helped me bury her. The dust storm had passed. We lifted her body into the handcart and pulled it across the desolate fields between the farms to the place.

The graveyard was at the back of Otto's hay barn, a place so situated that the dust rarely gathered there, the place where Otto and Greta had buried their son a year earlier. So we dug a second grave, Mary's grave. I dug and dug without stopping. I put all I had left into the digging of her grave. I dug so that she would not lie in a shallow place but deep in the cool hard ground beneath the dust. I did not, could not stop for water, or for the milk Greta brought. Sweat poured from my body as I dug. Tears stayed fast. It was too hard a thing for tears and besides I would need to be alone to cry. I would not cry. Otto cried, Greta cried. There was their son to think of. He had been nine years and four months when the pneumonia from the dust had taken him, but I had my child, a living, motherless child to think of, to care for.

When the grave was finished and Mary's body laid in it, we

stood around it: Otto, Greta, their daughter Leah, myself with the child in my arms. Otto spoke, I could not. He read from his bible about the life everlasting and the resurrection but his words were lost to me and I found no comfort in them.

I left the child with Greta and went home across the fields. Otto came with me. I gave him the milk cow and the chickens and a pig barely fit for slaughter. For myself I gathered little other than a knife, a water bottle and a change of clothes. I stood in our bedroom, the room where Mary had died, and took a last look. My eyes lighted on the small table beside the bed, where the lamp sat. Mary's bible was there. I picked it up and pushed it into the cloth bag that held my few possessions and left. The house and everything in it was as tinder. It took in an instant. When I looked back, the flames were already licking the sky.

18

Highway 66. The world moving west. We were set fast for the promised land. The land of plenty away from a world turned to dust and the wind howling up out of Texas. California was on our minds. Day and night a caravan of people, a great exodus rolling westwards. People who had sold up, burned up, loaded what few possessions they had remaining onto their makeshift trucks and headed off in search of a new life, a better life.

They needed men for the harvest. They spent enough of their riches telling us so what with the posters and the flyers – *Fruit Pickers Wanted – 5,000 families needed, Cabins and Tents Free* – we had all seen them. So when we saw the men coming back, men who had made it to the border and beyond, when they told us it was all a lie, we didn't believe them. We had to see for ourselves. We had to know different.

Having no truck, I hitched my way west. There was always someone willing to pick me up and take me to the next roadside camp but mostly I slept in ditches because it cost a half a dollar to stay in a camp where there was piped water and shade and it was money I didn't have. Camping on the roadside you risked being caught by the sheriff. They were all for moving you on. They didn't want this army of people invading their world. It was hard enough for them. The whole country was suffering and there was nothing the likes of us could do about it. The whole country was on the move, or so it seemed then.

It was the thought of the child, Eloise, that kept me moving. The child with Otto and Greta. I hadn't thought to be a man who could leave his own child but they persuaded me, or so I liked to think. I could go for the harvest, plenty had, and earn money. It could help us all. They would look after her and she would be waiting when I got back. A short while, a year or two, no more. It would be nothing in a child's life, they said. But to tell the truth, I was too easily persuaded. It was as if feeling had left, as if every part of me was numb and so it remained. A man cannot lose his livelihood, abandon his child, bury the the woman he loves most in this world without growing a new skin, a skin as thick and hard and cold as the winter ice.

It was as they promised, lush and green, a garden filled with willow, walnut and all manner of fruit and vegetables. Oranges hung plenty and rich from the trees but if you picked one you were liable to be shot, no matter that your belly was stuck with hunger or your child was starving, no matter that you'd come through the desert.

We were miserable and hungry, dirty and ragged. We were their people but they were afraid of us. At the borders they sent guards to turn us back. 'Go home, there's nothing for you here,' they said. What did they know of where we'd come from? I heard tell of plenty who refused to be persuaded back, just driven right on, but then in time they brought out their guns.

I came in alone under nightfall across the Yuma bridge and before long I was picking for twenty cents a day plus biscuits and living in a camp. I wrote to Greta and Otto. I said I hoped they were well and that Eloise was coming on as a child should. I told them I was looking for work. That I hoped to send money very soon.

I shared a tent with two others. I met them in the fields.

Chester was a young man, barely above sixteen, left his family back in Oklahoma working the land like Otto and Greta. Chester was all set to make a better life for himself. Frank was older, had little to say and looked to me like a dead man walking, like the journey had sucked the life from him.

Nights by the fire, I would talk with Chester about the land. How here there was land a plenty. How we could not take our eyes off it and we could not help but covet it. All our talk was of what we could do with just one piece, just one morsel of that land. Frank said nothing, just coughed the cough I knew.

The camp was filthy, plagued with lice and all manner of disease and not everybody was fortunate enough to have a tent. They lived under carpets, in cardboard boxes, beneath sheets of corrugated iron. Many of them were families with small children and old folks in tow. We took what work we could even though it wasn't enough to keep one man alive let alone a whole family but we helped each other out. We relied on charity and goodwill. Although it often appeared as if they were against us, not all Californians wished us ill.

We worked hard for six weeks until the harvest was in, then no more. They discarded us like rotten fruit and I could not see how I would ever work to earn enough money to send back to Otto and Greta. The future looked black as dirt. East the land was ruined. West the land would never belong to us. Word was there was work north, picking cotton. I was thinking to find me something, anything to make it worthwhile, so there was money left over to send back to Otto. I would go north. I told Chester and he was all for coming with me, but we hadn't reckoned with the Department of Health.

They came by night, the men in their blue Department of Health jackets and helmets, armed and with their dogs which I swear were as hungry as we were. Their purpose, to move us on. No matter that it was dark and children were sleeping. They turned their searchlights on the camp, sweeping across it and hailed us through their loudspeakers. There was no hiding place. Half an hour was what they gave us. We had half an hour to gather what little we possessed before they would douse the place and set it alight. Chester and me would have been long gone, me having precious little but my rags and Mary's bible, and Chester likewise, but a wind sprung up out of nowhere and the old woman set up moaning and I saw the fear on her son's face.

They were camped right next to our tent. The Parker family, decent people out of Missouri. There were six of them and that included the grandmother, Lillian, and she was sick near to death, been like it for days, stretched out, lying silent on an old mattress and them with no money to fetch a doctor. Now she was moaning bad and the searchlights were right over us and the dogs barking and straining at the leash. I went over and set about helping Jed Parker load the truck and move the old woman while Chester helped the rest of the family gather their belongings and pile them in the back of their old jalopy.

Between me and Jed we lifted the mattress. We put her in the back of the truck with the kids and the pots, pans and pillows. Jed told us to climb up with the kids and take a ride with them to the next camp at least and we were glad of that. Only the truck wouldn't start and before we knew it the half hour was up and they lit the first fire. I was at the front under the hood, looking to see if the fan belt might be busted when the fire took hold. That first fire was mostly cardboard. It was close by and in no time the wind whipped up the flames. Sparks flew in all directions, like a great firework display. Jed shouted at the family to get out of the truck and start running. Chester helped Jed's wife and the young ones while Jed shouted for me to help him with the old woman.

'Help me lift her. On my back,' he screamed. But before we could get a hold of the mattress the wind blew a spark that caught it and engulfed her in fire. He grabbed her feet and pulled her body from the truck but it was already too late.

When we stood in the roadside ditch, huddled together out

of fear and loathing and against the wind, watching the flames destroy the camp, I knew it was over. It was enough. My world had turned from dust to fire. I grant you the first was set by my own hand. It was of my own making. The second was something I never thought to witness. Nor to hear a man howl like a coyote as we dragged him away from the blackened corpse of his very own flesh and blood.

That night, the dream of the West turned as sour as the green fruit on its trees. In the morning I told Chester I wished him well but had determined to make my way back.

Weeks stretched into months on the road. I'd heard nothing from Otto and Greta. I kept myself going by imagining my homecoming, the surprise on their faces when they found me on the stoop. I comforted myself by trying to picture the child and by reading Mary's bible. The word on the road was that the storms were worsening. The newspapers were calling it Black Sunday, April 15. *Daylight Turns to Inky Blackness as Duster Hits*, read the headlines. By all accounts it came out of the north-east an hour before sunset and some folks were left thinking it must be the end of the world. A midnight blackness, they said. I read it all, but dust or no dust I was not for turning back. I carried on against the tide of humanity sweeping west, until that is, I came upon Mary's cousin, Amos Jones.

Amos was camped out by the road with his wife Bethany, his three sons, and their old jalopy piled high with all their worldly goods. I recognised him straight away. I knew him from Sunday church and from the farmers' meet. His tall frame and his corn blonde hair were unmistakable. No need to wonder or ask where they were travelling to or why.

He didn't recognise me. I saw that in his eyes. I saw the bewilderment as I walked towards him with my hand out. It was a long time since I'd looked in a mirror or seen my reflection but I knew how my clothes hung from me and how my hair was longer than it should be. I hesitated but then I saw recognition dawn, then shock which he did his best to hide.

'Silas, well, I'll be damned,' he said and he shook my hand. 'How you doing, Silas?'

'Surviving,' I said, 'surviving, just. On my way back as it happens, to Otto's and Greta's. I sure will be glad when I get there.'

His chest lifted with a sharp in breath. He leaned back from me and I saw the regret for what he was about to say.

'Well now, there's a thing, Silas, because as far as I know, they're on their way out to meet you. Last I knew they'd given up the farm. Sold what they could.Why, we bought the horse and trap off them, only the horse died.'

A heaviness came over me then and made its way through my body down to my broken shoes and out to the earth. 'Are you sure?' I asked. I looked hard into Amos's eyes, blue as a California sky. 'Are you sure?'

'I'm afraid so, Silas,' he said.

I sank to my knees. In that moment I could see no way of ever being re-united with my daughter and as God is my witness I wished with all my being that I had died and been buried with Mary at the back of Otto's barn. Amos helped me up and Bethany made me black tea. I sat with them awhile by the roadside. They did their best to persuade me to go with them. What was the point in going back, Amos said. He was sure we could find Greta and Otto. He was still full of the hope we'd all had before we set out. I warned him, of course. I told him just as others had told me about the life out West. He didn't believe me. How could he? He had staked everything on this new land. He had to go see for himself. When we parted company I wished them well.

Aiyana

19

December. Snow Moon. Silas be gone out hunting when I wake. I tell by the light it be the first snow of winter, the doe season. Hunting easy in the snow, tracks say follow me. Silas out there with Floyd, all the men out there, guns burning holes in the doe flesh, blood on the snow. I wrap myself in the blanket and go stand on the deck, look at the world now it be white and soft like it drip cotton, like it Christmas already. I thinking of Christmas. No December, still no Lyle and no word from Hetty. Sometimes the river sing a lonely song. Only one thing change now, I ain't so lonely. I got the words.

Guns crack in the woods, doe frightened, skitter through the trees, running from their bullets. Running from Floyd and from Silas. They a match for each other, what with their cruelties, got no thought for what they do to mama or me. Hunt women like they do the doe. Only the doe they kill there and then, spill her innards on the snow. Women they kill slow, trail of blood drip, dripping, up to the mountains and far down to the sea.

If I am not careful I will turn into mama, waste my days, waste whole springs, whole summers, a whole life sitting, drifting, eyes dead, lips not daring to move. But I got anger too much for that. Got anger like rock in my heart, ain't letting go. I let go and I be done for, dead as the doe. I am storing up my anger, holding on, chest tight, skin stretched out and drying in a fierce sun. I am keeping it to myself til the time come right.

I ain't the only one feel this way about Floyd and Silas. Seem to me there only Hannah who like Floyd and she as lonely as a fawn lost its mother. Silas got no one. Nobody like them, even the men they out hunting with, they just scared of them. Grandma say there be a time when the hunter offer up his thanks to the doe for her meat, the meat that feed us through the frozen moons of winter. Not these men. Not Floyd. He lost all respect. Only thinking of himself. It end badly, grandma say, and I reckon she be right. Ain't nobody prosper when he ain't got respect for others.

I go inside, get dressed for outdoors, feed the stove, tie up my boots and my coat. Hannah is expecting me. She say come early while the men be out hunting. I put my book and my brown papers in a flour sack bag, push them down in my coat pocket. It ain't Hetty's old orange book. It ain't *Dick and Jane*, I been working hard with Hannah and I already past all that. I past *come* and *go* and *play* and *dog*. Past *this* and *that*. About ready to leap out the orange book to any book you care to name. I learning quick. Even Hannah surprised how quick I learning.

Got my book from the Store. Buy it with some of the button money I been saving for me and December. Got no use for that money now, besides there plenty more where it come from, always be buttons to collect. And if I learn to read, well who knows I get out of here and I find him. I find December for sure and we make a life together and we don't need no button money. There also be my daddy to think of. My real daddy. Maybe it's possible, if I look hard enough, I find him too.

I buy me a book of clean pages. It ain't bible big, is small, got a blue cover, got a border and a place for writing your name, only I ain't writing it yet on account of being afraid somebody find it. I put my paper with the letters of the alphabet in the back. Hannah write words for me to copy in the front. Keep it under the mattress. I hurry to Hannah's, guns firing in the woods, boots leaving hollows in the snow. Fire sound like it getting nearer, wonder should I go? But she say come and I won't be missing one day of learning.

I am snow woman, purple shadow, hawk hanging in the trees, ice in my lungs, breath sharp, wary of the dogs, til I reach the twisted willow. Hannah waiting. She make coffee already. Say do I want honey cake, she make it like her mama's recipe. I look up at the photograph on the wall, her mama don't look like a woman make cake to me, she look like a woman chase you off her boat and beat you with a stick. I say, thank you, but I ain't hungry. I want to start. Get my books from my pocket, put them on the table. But Hannah go over to where the gramophone stand, open a drawer and bring out another book. She put it down in front of me.

'This is what we will read today, Aiyana. Today a real book. You are ready. It is the best way.' The cover is green and gold, got a picture of a boy on it, a boy like Lyle, with a fishing rod. She point at the words: *The Adventures of Tom Sawyer, Mark Twain*, she say. And she open the book and she start to read.

'Chapter One. "Tom!" No answer. "Tom!" No answer. "What's gone with that boy I wonder? You Tom!"'

Then she look at me and she say it be my turn. Put my finger by each word, make the sounds. Sometimes I guess, sometimes it's not so hard to tell what's coming next. I look at Hannah then and she nod or if I don't know the word, she whisper it and I say it after her. And that's how we go on, line by line with *The Adventures of Tom Sawyer*.

Hannah is a good teacher, she be patient. I am not so scared of her now, is like she be different. It like she want to help me, like she just as lonely as mama and me. Hannah Lutz got her own lonely river song. It's on her lips, in her smile, the way she get pleased when I am reading good, like she done something good too.

I am slow. I am not sure of the words but I be sure of one thing, the sticks on the page, the marks and shapes like nothing I know, they starting to look different. They ain't the puzzle they used to be. They starting to make a whole lot more sense.

We up to where Tom's aunt about to give him a beating when the guns sound loud, like they be on our backs.

'Quickly,' she say. 'It is time you were not here. The men are coming home. Here, take this.' She hand me *The Adventures of Tom Sawyer*. 'For you.'

'For me?'

'Yes, you, go on, take it, Aiyana. I want you to have it.'

I thank her. Wish I could find a way to say I understand how she be feeling. A way to tell her I am missing him and grieving too but it seem too hard so I just pack my books in the flour sack bag.

'Hurry,' she say.

I am gone.

Hurry through the snow but it slow me down. I am late. When I get to the boat Silas is already waiting, sitting at the table and he ain't got his bible, he just sitting waiting like he been watching the door for me coming in. He ain't pleased. 'Where have you been?' He say in that cold way of his, like he judge and jury and he ain't thinking of mercy. 'What's that in your pocket?'

'Nothing,' I say. 'I just been to mama's.'

'Nothing. Sure looks like something to me. Mama's you say? That's not what your footprints say. They lead in the opposite direction.'

'Been to Hannah's too. She tell me to come, give me some brown paper from the Store for wrapping the doe meat, smoked fish and the like, that's all.' I am busy unbuttoning my coat, unlacing my boots, bending down, hoping he don't see my face. 'You hungry? Want coffee? Hunting good?'

'Leave your coat and your boots. There's meat enough and there's work for you, skinning and the like, your daddy's waiting. Empty your pocket before you go. Put the paper on the table.'

I never been much good at lying. He see through me. I am

115

as dead as the doe waiting to be skinned. He knows he got me.

'Hurry up,' he say.

'Might as well take it with me, be useful for wrapping.' I put my hand over the flour sack bag in my pocket, feel the corners of *Tom Sawyer* under my fingers.

'Let me see.' He getting up from the table. He grab my arm and pull my hand out my pocket. Then he take the bag and open it. He look at *The Adventures of Tom Sawyer,* he look at me like he puzzle. Then he open the exercise book and see the writing and flick the pages. His face grow dark. Alphabet pages fall out on the table. He turn them over and then the storm come. 'As God is my witness you are a liar. You know fine well your father has forbidden this.' He turn his back to me. Walk over to the stove, open the front, rattle the logs with the iron, make the flames leap, then he take my alphabet pages and feed them to fire one by one. Now he is ripping up my exercise book. Do the same with that.

'Please, Silas, I beg you don't, please don't. There ain't no harm in it. I just want to know the word. Surely everyone's got a right to reading and writing. I'm begging you, Silas, please.' I grab his arm, pull it back from the stove. He turn at me, flames in his eyes. Fire in him now. He push me down onto the floor. His boot press on my chest and river water come flooding up to my lungs. I am fighting for my breath. Lie there and watch as he pick up *The Adventures of Tom Sawyer*.

He about to put it to the fire when I hear the echo of footsteps on the gangplank. Hear the barking of a dog. I think I know that dog. I know those footsteps. Then the door burst open and who be standing there but Lyle. It is Lyle, and Castor be at his side low growling like the wolf. Silas take one look and he put the book down, grab his coat and fly off. I never been so pleased in all my life to see my brother Lyle as I am now.

Silas

20

I was forty miles west of Amarillo, at a dusty crossroads, heading east through Texas when I came upon them. The bay was tethered in the shade of an oak. The wagon was brightly painted, though the paint was flaked and worn. His name was written across it in faded gold letters. *Doctor Hangood* – and in red letters beneath – *The people's physician, here to ease your suffering. Alchemist of well-being, purveyor of remedies.*

Clouds of children hovered like mosquitos around the wagon. There were automobiles too and trailers parked nearby. Flyers promised live entertainment – *Chief Thundercloud and the trail of tears, Hermann the Great: magician extraordinaire, Madame Blanche: foreteller of crops and romance,* and a museum of curiosities including anatomical charts, shrunken heads, exotic butterflies and a pickled foetus.

A crowd had assembled, as always does when there's a travelling show in town. Mostly they were corn shuckers and cowboys, melon growers too for the fields were ripe with them and their wives and children. It was good to be among people. I was weary of my own company. I'd had too much of it for people had begun to avoid me. I saw it in their eyes, I was not to be trusted, a single man, wanderer, unkempt, unwashed. A hollow-eyed scavenger is what I'd become and I wasn't above stealing or doing others out of what was theirs because I had lost all hope, all hope of meeting Otto and Greta and of seeing my daughter. A mountain of loss can turn a man into something other than himself.

Doc Hangood, as I came to know him, was soon addressing the crowd. He stepped down from the wagon onto a hastily erected stage, doffed his frayed top hat, smoothed his hand down his red brocade waistcoat, cleared his throat and raised his right arm in a form of salute: 'Afternoon, ladies and gentlemen, dear friends, discerning folk – welcome. Knowledgeable as you are in matters pertaining to necessary remedies and lifelong health, welcome to our extravaganza of entertainment, Doc Hangood's travelling show, up from Louisiana, via the great Colorado river. We are here to offer you not only the elixir of life, the remedy to surpass all remedies, a herbal preparation from the King's American Dispensatory of 1898 but with our own special and particular ingredient, a secret known only to myself and my trusted helpers. No, eager though you may be, my friends, this can wait. My remedies for what presently ails you, you can buy all in good time. First, for your entertainment, before I dispense the very first bottle, music, there will be music to raise the spirits. Iry Benoir and his brother, Henry, will play for you on the finest fiddle and banjo known to man, handcrafted from maple. Please welcome them now, welcome them as only big-hearted Texans can. Ladies and gentlemen, put your hands together for the Benoir brothers.'

The music both enlivened and softened the crowd. A queue formed for card readings and for the pulling dentist who sat you on his chair and extracted your troublesome tooth. By the time Doc Hangood was ready to sell his brown bottle elixir they needed little convincing and if they needed any, there were several in the crowd willing to step up and give testimony. They were Doc Hangood's shills, men and women enlisted to encourage sales, and when I saw them, I saw my opportunity. Before the day was out I had approached one. He was smoking under the oak where the bay was tethered, a man who had earlier held his withered arm aloft and waved it about claiming

Doc Hangood's remedy had put life back in his unfortunate limb. His name was Aaron. I told him I needed work, and by nightfall, when the travelling show made its hasty getaway to avoid complaints or demands for refunds or the attention of the sheriff, I was given clean overalls and a decent meal and I joined them on the road.

I suppose you could say I was grieving for company and the chance to feel half human. It seemed to me there was warmth by their campfire. There were no questions asked about the past or future. The men and women of Doc Hangood's travelling show knew acceptance if nothing else. At a time when half the world seemed to be on the move, on the road or riding the rails, a time where I had little hope or intention for my future, I was happy to be on the move too.

Doc Hangood was a man of conflicting mood. He was fearsome when in preaching mode and he could roll his eyes to the back of his head at will. He was fickle. If well-inclined he would overpay and order extra rations in for the crew. If displeased he would lash out for the slightest misdemeanour. I knew well by now how to keep my own counsel and I kept out of the Doc's way. Aaron, the man with the unfortunate limb, was my only confidante. He was a sharecropper rendered homeless by the death of his mother after which he'd taken to the road where he'd found a home with Doc Hangood. I told him that I was heading home even though I expected to find little or nothing to salvage. I told him about Otto and Greta and how I suspected that, like me and thousands of others, they would see their dreams of a new life dashed and if I knew Otto, he would want to make his way back. His father, like mine, had put his heart into that land. It was not something to be relinquished.

I saw out the summer and fall with Doc Hangood's travelling show. It was easy and companionable and it took my mind off my sorrows. I grew strong again being properly fed and watered like the bay Aaron took care of. The show travelled south to see out the worst of the winter but it was a cold spring later when I found myself cut adrift and a long way from home.

Good things rarely last as I was well versed in understanding. We had ventured into the state of Arkansas. We arrived in a small town square. I do not recall its name and we were barely begun when the law men moved right in, like they'd planned it good and proper. Doc Hangood was arrested there and then in front of the crowd and taken off in handcuffs and locked up in the town jail on a charge of purveying fraudulent goods. The crowd booed and hissed and we scattered each in our own direction for fear of being arrested too.

My spirits were low. I had lost the companionship of Aaron and the quiet passage of our days. I slept alone. The spring was cold and the wind out of the north unforgiving. I determined that the very next day I would ride out of Arkansas on the rails and make the journey back home to the farm as quickly as I could. I had bedded down for the night close to the river in a hollow, covering myself in newspaper and what leaves I could gather from the winter ground, when I heard the voices. At first they were less than distinct, disguised by the wind, but as the men grew closer they became louder and those voices were angry. I lifted myself up from my bed, keeping my head down, and saw the outlines of two men, one fatter than a man should be in lean times and the other broad shouldered and thick necked, walking through the trees towards where I'd settled for the night.

'We agreed the price, thirty dollars for three days fishing and now you're asking me for nearly twice that amount. Money I haven't got. Ten a day we agreed and ten it is and not a cent more, you hear me?' It was the fat man.

'Well now, my recollection was fifteen dollars a day plus expenses. And that comes to at the very least forty five dollars. So we'll call it fifty and I reckon you pay me what you owe me like an honest man and be done with it. It's late now and I'm fixing to get home and eat my supper.' The younger man, carrying the fishing tackle, stopped in front of the fat man. I could just make out the rods and seine nets in the gathering dusk. He turned to face him. 'I ain't arguing,' he said. 'Pay up now before we reach the truck and that's the last you'll see of me.'

'I ain't paying you nothing.' The fat man attempted to push past. A scuffle ensued. Both men were on the floor, edging closer to my nest and leaves and I saw the fat man reaching for his gun. 'Look out, he's got a gun,' I shouted.

The younger man's head turned rapidly in my direction and then rapidly back. He flung himself at the fat man, took the gun and grabbed him by the throat. By the time I was up and out of the hollow he had pulled a knife and the fat man was a squealing pig for the sticking. Blood leached and pooled on to the hard ground and before I knew it I was helping the younger man, who I guessed to be of a similar age to myself, drag the body to the river and set the corpse on its journey down to the Mississippi. But not before the fat man's pockets were emptied. I wanted none of his money but the younger man insisted and pushed two hundred dollar bills into my hand.

'Banker,' he said as we heaved the body into the icy water. 'No good rich banker, the world's better off without the likes of him. I'm Floyd Weir, by the way. Pleased to make your acquaintance.' He held out his hand, then seeing it was bloody, bent to wash the blood in the river water. I did the same. 'It's mighty cold for a man to be sleeping in the woods. Where you headed anyways?'

'Been to California, heading back to Oklahoma. It's a long story.'

'I do believe you're a mighty long way from home. I live a mile or so upstream on the river. Best you come home with me and you can tell me that story while we're walking. There's food and a bed on the floor at least. My family is there, got me two fine daughters. Appreciate it greatly if you would see your way to accepting our hospitality and this here show tonight, well, I'd appreciate it greatly if it just stay between us.'

I nodded. Floyd Weir was not a man to argue with. I'd seen the proof with my own eyes. He was a man who thought nothing of taking another's life. A man who smelled of fish and river water and blood money. His lust for blood sat there in his eyes, shining through the dark. I felt his power then and for the first time since I'd buried Mary I felt truly alive. Power surged through my veins like I'd swallowed every bottle of Doc Hangood's elixir and been reborn.

The man we'd heaved into the water was nothing but a fat greedy banker on his way to the Delta. Hadn't bankers been the cause of all our downfall? He'd deserved what he got, he had it coming. If he'd paid up, if he'd paid what he promised he'd still be alive but greed had got the better of him. And the promise of food and warmth and a bed to lie on and the dollars in my pocket had got the better of me.

As we walked through the dark towards Floyd Weir's riverboat home I felt the weight of Mary's bible in my pack and wondered what I'd come to.

She was a beauty, black-eyed and honey skinned and from the moment I saw her I couldn't take my eyes from her. Hetty Weir, promised to Johnson Crawford, sat at the meagre table on her father's boat and the light from the kerosene lamp fell on her face and despite myself, and in that very moment, I fell in love. I did not believe in a man falling in love at first sight. It wasn't practical. It wasn't how I had lived but I hadn't reckoned for Hetty. I'd loved Mary for her goodness and her care but Hetty lit a fire in me. She had that same charge and power that her father Floyd had. They were people used to getting what they wanted. I hesitate to say immoral but in time that's how I came to think of Floyd, and Hetty. The difference was Hetty had a conscience, something that Floyd seemed to know nothing of.

She was the eldest child. She took after her mother in looks;

half native and must have been a beauty although the light had gone from her and she was prematurely old, or that's how it seemed to me that first night and I had little reason to change my view.

As for the rest of the family, the twins were but children and I preferred not to think too much of them because they reminded me of Eloise. The boy, Lyle, was suspicious from the start. His eyes challenged me. He had the sense that we'd been up to no good and his dog sensed the same. That dog never did do anything other than growl at me.

Aiyana was Floyd's whipping post. He beat her at will and half drowned her, trying to subdue her spirit. She too was a beauty, not that she appeared to have an inkling of that. Her health was not good and she hadn't attended school like the others. The child could not read.

I had no thought of staying when I went home that night with Floyd but by the next morning when Hetty made me coffee and raised her smile at me, I was no longer in a hurry to leave.

Hetty was used to getting what she wanted. Towards her father she breathed defiance. Any fear she might have had of Floyd Weir, and which the others clearly demonstrated, she'd grown out of. Her every move said: don't touch me. But when she looked at me as she did that morning, it was a different message I read. It was a look that said maybe, just maybe, you may touch me. It was a look that teased and hypnotised and it made me forget all about my intentions of going home.

I made efforts to resist Hetty's lure and Floyd's grip. I read Mary's bible nightly in the hope that it would guide me and save my soul. But I was weak and all the while I slipped further into sin until I became the man I am now. Souls are not saved by good intentions.

It was Floyd who said I should stay and make a life on the river where there was food and fish a plenty, the means of a man making a living without perpetual struggle. There was moonshine at night, fishing and hunting by day. I guess he was all for keeping me close by, what with me knowing how he'd knifed the banker without a second thought. And before long the Sheriff came around poking his nose in, asking questions. Seems the body got washed up down river and they were after whoever did the killing. So I became Floyd's alibi and he wanted to keep me sweet.

It was Floyd who suggested I do up Rockwell's old boat. Chances were, he said, that Hetty would change her mind about Johnson and that way there'd be room for me to start courting her. I figured I had nothing to lose. I had dollars in my pocket, the money to get me what I needed to do up the boat and make me a decent home. But it was the girl I wanted and the more I watched her, the more I wanted her. And that wanting never stopped right up to her wedding day and beyond. It never changed, and the want was an ache no amount of bible reading could cure.

I painted the boat green for her. It got so she would appear there most days while I worked and before long we were taking what chance we could to be alone. We were planning on being together. She would tell Johnson it was over and after a suitable time we would be married. But Johnson got wind of it and went to see Floyd.

I didn't find out until later what Johnson had on Floyd, though I knew it had to be a powerful thing. Elmer Glass, the old outlaw who brewed the moonshine, let it slip one night when he had too much of his own medicine. It was something Hetty had told Johnson, something if I'd known at the time I might have acted on. If I'd known Floyd Weir had forced himself on his own daughter, on Hetty, I might have killed him. Instead I sat by while he ordered her to marry Johnson and beat her half to death. For once she took that beating. I guess two men willing to take whatever they wanted, with no thought for her or her feeling, finally broke her spirit.

I might have taken her away with me then, only weeks before

the wedding. I was thinking of it the night I met her on the Bluff. I was planning our escape but when she told me she was with child and the child was mine, I knew it was over. The road was no place for a woman in her condition and I could not put her in danger.

Aiyana

21

Birds shaking snow from the cottonwoods, falling like spring blossom, smell of blood on the wind. Boots snow-heavy, walking towards Floyd, my breath short still, even though Lyle draw me a cup of water, even though he say we wait until my lungs empty and breath come back, even though Castor lick my face and my hands like he never forget me.

'Where's that boy?' He ask. 'He hiding behind you in them trees? Got that good for nothing, flea ridden dog of his with him?'

'He gone.' I say. 'Ain't coming back.'

Floyd stand on the bank, got an axe in his hand, the dead doe and her young lie on the sledge, snow spots settle their skin. A buck hang from a low branch, tip of his antlers touching the ground. Mama and Ada got their skinning knives out, they cutting and scraping skin from the flesh, cut then rip, part the skin from the white, fur from the flesh, tear down. Buck is raw, he purple and red, stripped to his meat. Silas sit on the log pile smoking, watching, eyes on me.

'You are lying,' say Floyd. 'Don't lie to me. Now, where's that boy? When I find him and I will, you can be sure of that, I gonna show him what happens to cowards and runaways.'

'Is true. I swear, he already gone, back across the rail yard, gonna jump a train down to the Delta, got him a job waiting.' I look at mama. She stop skinning, turn away from the buck, face slipping, got that sadness creeping over her. She put her knife on the sledge and go back down to the boat. I know she always hoping to see him. He like her fawn, lost in the winter woods. Now her hope lost too.

'Why did he come back then, if he got himself a job and all, what reason has he got for coming back here? Tell me that?'

'Don't know. Guess he just want to know we still here, see us, see his home one last time.' Floyd looking at me like he ain't sure. I am trying hard not to let the liar's heat creep up my face. Silas drop his cigarette butt on the floor and grind it under his boot even though the snow do the job for him. He burn me with his look. I reckon he not sure either. I hold my ground. What choice they got but to believe me? Lying getting to be my habit. Almost believe myself.

Floyd pick up mama's knife, take it over to the buck and start skinning and ripping. His back is to me, and he say in a low voice, 'You stay away from Hannah Lutz. No good come of her learning you nothing. You hear me?'

'I hear you.' I look across at Silas, he put his head down. I put my head down, walk to the gangplank. Wood wet slipping under my feet.

Inside, mama is sitting at the table. She look at me like she hoping a miracle come along, like Lyle gonna appear right now.

'How did he look?' She ask me.

'He look just fine, mama.' There I go lying again but ain't no way I tell her his clothes all holes and rags and his bones poking through. 'He say to tell you he be just fine and you ain't to worry about a thing. He got work waiting in New Orleans. He on his way there now.'

She sigh. 'Sent me a postcard. Sent it to Ada. I was about to show you when daddy came back. Ada read it to me, said he was thinking of coming home for Christmas. Now he's been and gone already and I didn't so much as catch a glimpse of him. Not one look.'

She near to crying I tell. 'He was hoping to see you, mama,

is why he came but you know how it is, what with daddy. Was hoping he catch me by myself but once Silas see him he know he have to go.'

She nod her head. 'I guess so. I'm glad to know he's safe and well and out of here and that's a fact but I would have liked to have just one look at him, just one.'

She go quiet then. We drink coffee. Boat rock gently, we both thinking of Lyle. Is peaceful for a while until Floyd start shouting for me to come up. He want me to skin the fawn. His voice sound like a hammer in my head. I think on that night, smell his moonshine breath. Think of how the wolf save me. I full to bursting with hatred for Floyd Weir, swear I could take that skinning knife and put it right through his heart.

I pick up a pan of soup been sitting by the stove. 'Gonna take this to grandma,' I say to mama. She don't answer, she still lost in her thoughts. I go outside. He see me, expecting me to come help. 'Mama want me to take this to grandma.' I don't look at him, or Silas, or the hanging deer or the blood red snow. Climb in the rowboat and cross the river.

Grandma already know about Lyle, reckon she seen his tracks. 'Where is he?' She whisper as I hand her the soup.

'Hiding, up in the woods, near the Bluff, that old fisherman's cabin. He half-starved and Castor too. They be needing food badly, need blankets to keep them from the cold. But I scared Floyd or Silas see me go.'

'Let me think now, little one. The trouble is if Floyd see me go it will be equally bad. We must be careful, Wild Plum. We must be silent as the wolf. Night is the time, darkness will give us cover. Floyd Weir has to sleep sometime, that man of yours too.'

'He ain't my man.'

'I know, child. Now, I will get everything Lyle needs and you will take it up river when they are sleeping. I will be waiting. I will stay up with the owls, eyes wide, ears pricked for the ripples on the water. I will smell your boat on the wind.

And I will watch for you coming back. I will burn sweetgrass and tobacco for your safe return.'

Silas smell of sinew, of muscle and flesh. Scrub his hand and nails like he always do then take out his bible and sit reading and he don't say a word to me, just hang his head until he go to blow out the lamp and say it be time for sleep. I say I still got chores and I need a wash. Tell him to take the bed and I sleep on the boards. He don't disagree, just look at me, then turn and go to the bedroom. I sit by the lamp and wait for his breath coming heavy as it do in sleep. Then, when I sure he be sleeping and he ain't gonna wake, take my coat and boots and creep out into the night.

Snow hard on the ground, breath frost in the air. The sky be ink and a snow moon drift in and out of the cloud. I row on the black water, soft oars dipping, silent as I can. Grandma waiting, like she say. I tell by the smell of burning tobacco. We ain't speaking none but when I get close she just lower the food in a basket, and a bundle of fur and blankets too.

I row up river to the Bluff, past mama's boat, keep my head low and my oars soft. Eyes sieving the dark, praying it be only me and the screech owl and the possum. Pray Lyle still be there like he say. I promise him to come but who knows, maybe he give up hope.

I pull into the bank and fasten the boat. Take the bundles, climb up the back of the Bluff, whistle like a green frog when I get close to the cabin. Nothing. Whistle again. Whistle three times then a low growling come back. It's Castor, alright. I am outside the cabin door when it open and Lyle standing there. He shivering, white face in the night. Look like he brought back from the dead.

Inside the cabin it be dark except for a patch of moon through the high-up window. I light a candle from the basket. Lyle already eating the cornbread and dried fish. He drinking milk and he feed Castor too. I am putting the furs on the cabin floor. We sit down on them, blankets on our shoulders. Lyle ask me what happen.

I say, 'They believe me. He think you gone, mama too. Floyd still mighty upset with you. Only people know you be here, me and grandma.'

He don't say a word. I wonder what he think. Reckon he think it's impossible for him to stay, wonder why he come back at all. I am scared he is going already. 'You ain't going, Lyle, not when you only just come?'

'Ain't nothing for me here. Wait out the snow maybe and then I'm leaving.'

'If you go, then I am coming with you.'

'No, Aiyana. It's no life for a woman riding the rails. It's dangerous. No life for anyone.'

'But it is no life here. This time I go with you.'

He don't reply.

'You got my book?' I ask.

He reach over to the corner where his pack sit and pull something out. See the glint of gold on the cover. He hand me the book.

'Remind me of you with your fishing rod and all – *The Adventures of Lyle Weir* – I write it one day, you see.'

'Where'd it come from?'

'Hannah Lutz give it to me. She been teaching me to read, only I think is over now because Silas find out.'

'Hannah Lutz?' He look serious, his voice go quiet. His head go down and he reach for Castor and put his head on his fur. When he lift up and look at me, I see by his face in the candlelight it be something bad and I am afraid to my bones of what he about to say.

'Ain't no easy way to say this and I'm sorry as hell to be the messenger. But you got a right to know and it's partly why I came back. It's December. He ain't no more, Aiyana. December is gone. He is dead and no mistake. I saw his body myself on the rails.'

132

22

February. Hunger Moon. Snow melt, river running high and wild. Sorrow locked inside me. No one got the key. I cannot speak. Who to tell? Only the river and it's too full and too busy to care. I try to rise up and out with the eagle but my feet stay on the cold ground. Trees drip my snow tears. Lyle be long gone, he don't stay above three days and then he off. Seem like only yesterday he tell me. All this time I am thinking only one thing and that be December is dead. No matter if I leave this river, no matter how long a journey I make, I ain't never gonna see him again.

Before he go Lyle say that now I am reading he gonna write to me and tell me where he living, so I can join him when spring come. I beg Lyle to let me go with him. 'Please, Lyle, let me come now. I ain't staying here, it ain't possible. You the only hope I got.'

'I can't, Aiyana,' he say. 'It's nigh on freezing and your lungs they just ain't made for it. It's hard out there, men are dying of the cold and hunger. You got to stay here for now, but in the spring, then you come and I'll be waiting, find us some place to live and you never got to come back, ever.'

'What if Silas find out, or daddy?' I don't tell Lyle yet that Floyd ain't my daddy. There be plenty of time for that down the line. 'What if they be watching me every day and I never get away?'

'You'll find a way,' he say.

I tell him I am scared, beg him stay here through the winter. I will bring him food. I tell him he gotta stay, it ain't right not telling Hannah about December, she entitled to know and he be the one to do it. He say he ain't going near Hannah's boat on account of daddy might be there and besides she will know soon enough when the railroad officials send word. All my pleading like dead fish on the water. I know he gotta go. If he stay then sure as hell Floyd will find out.

I am glad he is gone now and that Floyd will not find him. About the only thing I am glad of. My heart be as heavy as the iron rails that December fall on. I am sleepwalking through my days.

Only one thing lift my spirits and that be my book. When I am sure Silas ain't around I take out *The Adventures of Tom Sawyer*, cry my tears on its pages, find my old notebook and my pencil, copy it out word for word. I say the words over and over, the ones I know. Ones I don't know I write in the back, saving them up, but for what I ain't sure. Reckon Hannah ain't gonna teach me no more. Floyd will see to it. He don't leave a stone like that unturned.

Boat rock in the winds. Is blanket cold, rooms icy, chill to the bone, fingers and toes numb, breath short. Silas bring deer meat and a stringer of catfish, he say I gotta eat but I ain't interested in food. Something's the matter, he know. He seem different. Like he care. Ask me what it is. 'Is it Lyle?'.

'No, it ain't Lyle.'

'What then? Are you sick, Aiyana?'

I nod.

'Where, where are you sick?'

'Is just my lungs.'

'You want me to fetch the doctor?'

'No, no doctor. I just sit a day or two by the stove and grandma make me a cure. Be fine then. You read your bible.'

I am the bird that cannot fly, dragging my wings on the forest floor. Silas see that. He see that much and he leave me be. Spend my days and nights thinking back to all the times I have with December. Only me and him. Conjure him like a spirit, feel him at my shoulder, breath on my neck, lips on my lips, like he be real. Like he be here with me now. Like he comfort me. Like he saying, 'Hush now, Aiyana, spring come soon and everything gonna be alright.'

Trouble is, he keep telling me it's time Hannah get to know. Thing like that can't be left to chance. He say I gotta tell her, ain't no railroad man coming. It be up to me.

It happens on a clear day. The winter sun is out. Fog and mist gone. Silas gone to work and mama is knocking on the boat door. 'Aiyana, come quickly, you gotta see this.' She sure is excited about something. Don't ever remember hearing her sound like this, like she a happy birthday child. 'Hurry now.'

I open the door and she standing there, coat and boots on, cheeks red from the cold. She got a look in her eye I only see when she talk about the past and she get that old photograph out.

'What is it, mama?' I ask.

'Put your coat and boots on, and follow me. You'll see soon enough.'

I do as she says and I follow her. She take the path by the river, out of the Creek where the river run wide and the sun firing up off the water. 'Look, there! You ever seen a boat as beautiful as that?'

And I gotta admit I ain't.

A long, wooden boat rests by the bank. It still have its sails up and they be red. The breeze catch them and the sun shine through them like they be alive. On the side it got words painted on it. One of the words got a *ph* at the beginning.

'Photographs,' say mama. I don't know how she know that word but she do.

It say, *Copying and Painting*, in big letters too on the side. I read them. Then something begin with *R*, I ain't sure of. The boat got six windows and four chimneys, thick boards and a painting of an angel on the side. Least, I think it be an angel, it look like a picture from a prayer book. And there is a name too, *E-L-L-A-P-F-R-Y,* but it's hard for me to make out.

A woman stands on board. She is tall, wearing a black coat, got a child in her arms that she set down and she put her hand up and fuss her hair which she got pinned up. Then she go and sit down at the back, got a bench there and she lift a book onto her lap. I see her open it and read.

Mama sigh, 'It's like the boat where my photograph was taken. Ain't exactly the same, this boat is more beautiful. I want you to have your photograph, Aiyana. But first you gotta get ready and you gotta promise me to smile.'

23

Wash my hair in nettle water, smooth it with the ivory comb Hetty give me. Go to the cottonwood chest and take out the only dress I got which look like it ain't made from cast offs and flour sacks. Is blue and it got a yellow collar. I dress myself. Lift out my purse of button money, there just a few cents left after I buy the paper and such. It got to be enough. Put the purse in a basket and cover it with a chequered cloth like I fetch bread in. Gonna get me a photograph like mama's.

I am first there, ain't nobody else come, not yet. The woman is washing pots, children playing in the mud. There be a man there too and he sitting at some kind of board and he got a paintbrush, look like he making a picture.

I call out, 'Morning, I hope I ain't disturbing you none.'

She stop washing pots, stand up tall and look out at me on the bank. The man act like he ain't heard.

'I am wondering if you might take my photograph? I got money with me.'

She nod, dry her hands on her apron, 'Come aboard.'

I step up onto the long plank, from riverbank to boat.

She lift a curtain at the door and show me the way through. Is a small room. Got a chair and the camera all set up, cotton sheet pinned on the wood, blue curtain across the window, sun shining at its back.

'Sit there, child, and rest your hands in your lap.'

Is peaceful, the boat shift in the tide, spill water rising underneath. Specks of dust floating like silk in the air.

'Now, you look this way, straight at the camera.'

I do as she ask, look at her, fold my hands in my lap.

She bend over, put her head under the black cloth then pull it back and stand up. 'You ain't quite right,' she say and come over, put her hands on my shoulders and move me in the seat. 'Why, child, your collar button is undone. Let me do it for you.' She go to do it up, then touch my back gentle as the breeze. 'What's this?' She ask.

I ain't knowing what to say. I try thinking up an excuse but she already undone three buttons at my dress back and she looking at the scars Floyd give me with his beatings. 'Who did this?' She ask, like she angry, like she care about my back, my old puckered skin.

'It ain't nothing.' I wanting her to take the photo, afraid I won't get one, afraid I will come away without a photo like mama's. Then there ain't no picture of me to prove what I be. 'Please,' I say. 'I gotta have the photo. Please.'

She do the buttons back up. 'What's your name, child?'

'Aiyana, like the wild plum.'

'Aiyana, that is a beautiful name,' she say. 'Now you look this way, Aiyana, and smile. You smile for all you're worth, child.'

I smile and the flash go off and light up the room. More than once. 'There. We gonna have a mighty fine photo for sure. Now, child, I got something for that back of yours. Old medicine for old scars but it sure do work well. My mother, Ella, swore by it. I'm named after her, Ella P. Fry. Pleased to make your acquaintance, Aiyana. Follow me now.'

And I do. I follow her to the kitchen, see the baby there lying in a rocking cradle. She shout out to the man on the deck, 'Don't you come on in here, Marvin, nor the young 'uns, don't go disturbing us while I see to this young lady's back.' A grunting noise come back which I think must be his way of saying he hear her.

138

'Don't mind him, child, bark worse than his bite for sure. He's a good man, never lifts a finger to the children and that's a fact. He lets me get on with the business of taking photographs. Don't interfere none, besides he's too busy with his pictures and all. He's good at it too, sells for a good price, keeps us afloat, anyway.'

She put the ointment on my back. It sting but I try not to show it. Tears pricking the back of my eyes, but it ain't the sting, it be kindliness make my tears come. She finish, do up the buttons, see my face, see my silent tears, they streaming now, ain't no stopping them.

'Hush now,' she say. 'I'm gonna make us a pot of fresh coffee and there's syrup biscuits I made only this morning. You gonna stay here with me, child, til I work out what to do.'

'I can't. I can't stay here. He will find me for sure and it be more trouble and I...'

'Hush, you stay awhile now, just for now.' She busy herself at the coffee pot.

Baby start complaining in his cot, he restless, wanting milk. I look at him, she look at me, 'Pick him up, why don't you? His name is Nathaniel. He always wants picking up. He is a troublesome child but he's mine.'

I pick up the baby, he be soft and warm skinned like babies be. I rock him.

I hear voices coming. I look from the window and see the queue. People coming to get their photograph, all in their Sunday best.

'Oh Lord,' she say, 'here already and the sun barely up. I got me some business. You look after the baby for me? Him out there, he ain't no use nor ornament when it comes to minding children.' Then she call out, 'Ruth! Jonah!'

The children come running in, reckon they be about five or six. They stare at me. 'Now don't pay Aiyana here any mind. She's gonna look after Nathaniel while I take the pictures. Get the tin, Ruth, and start collecting. Jonah, you give out the cards with the prices and the repairs on. Don't you forget to tell em how your pa repairs clocks and all.'

They nod. 'You be OK here with the baby? There's milk for him when he gets hungry in the cooling pan.'

'I be fine.'

Ruth empty the tin on the table and Ella counting the money. We drinking lemonade and she put her feet up on the kitchen stool. Baby asleep back in his cot and the children fishing down bank. Marvin stop painting and he asleep outside under his hat.

'Time I was gone, long gone. I got chores to do and Silas, if he find out I been away all day, no telling what he might do.'

'Is he your husband, child? You don't look near old enough to have a husband to me.'

'Not exactly,' I reply.

'Not exactly, now what does that mean?'

'I got given. My daddy give me to him. Lyle, he my brother, though he gone away, he say daddy sell me to him, to keep his mouth shut about things they been up to.'

'Uh huh,' say Ella and she nod like she getting the drift fast. 'And you don't get no say in the matter? What does your mama say?'

'Mama she don't say nothing. She know better than cross daddy. Me, I don't get no say on account of...' I stop. I am ashamed to say but Ella tell me, 'Go on, child.'

'On account of me never going to school and my lungs being full of river water and never learning to read and write like everyone else do. But I am learning now, only my teacher, well she ain't teaching me at this time. There be a problem with that. But one day I make my way out of here for sure. I ain't belonging to any man then, not Silas, not my daddy, not anyone.'

'Well now, I'm pleased to hear it. You've got spirit, child.

Now, we're fixing on being here a while before we go up river and I'm gonna need a child like you to look after the baby. I've got two of my own to teach and they are falling behind, make no mistake, so it would be a good thing if I did some learning with them and you could join in.'

'I could?'

'You could, child.'

'But if he find out, he...'

'If you slip down here early when he goes out, then back before he comes home, he won't know anything about it. It can be our secret. I am thinking you just might be the fastest learner I ever knew. I can show you the camera too and you can help me with the photographs. It's a good skill to have and a woman needs to earn her living in these times. I am in need of a young woman just like you. What do you say?'

'I know the alphabet. Some words too, like *photograph*. I know that.'

'Why, then you are already halfway there, child.'

Ella P. Fry, she true to her word. She teach me with the children and I help her. She say I already know a great deal when it come to the word, only trouble is we ain't got enough time. I am taking photographs too, the camera it comes easy to me.

But it ain't long enough. Even though she stay a week or more, it's nothing and I am sad as I ever be when she go but she tell me not to fret. I gotta keep watching and come spring I gonna see her red sails blowing back down the river. Ella say she come back for me.

I watch her go. Stand on the riverbank waving. She wave back and the children wave too. I watch them until they are out of sight, no sails on the river. Wonder if I will ever see her again. Think Ella P. Fry be the kindest person I ever met, apart from mama, and that be the truth. I give my photograph to mama for safe-keeping. She put it with hers. She says I am beautiful.

I say, 'I look like you.'

Whisper of hungry feet, feet that want something. Go to the door and she is already stepping off the bank onto the gangplank. There be no disguising Hannah Lutz. She tall, taller than most folk around here. Her hair curling from her woollen hat, hand clutch her coat to keep out the cold. She stop when she see me. Look around. Nobody about. River silent, river still, hungry as an old heron waiting for the catch.

'Come inside,' I say.

Inside she pull off her hat, shake her hair out. She be shivering. I go to the stove, open the front and put the pot on top to boil for coffee. 'Sit down, please.'

She sit.

'Is a risk, you coming here. If daddy get to know. He tell me I gotta stay away from you for good.' She nod. Rub her hands together. She nervous, I can tell. 'I still got the book though. Still got me Tom Sawyer, keep it under the bed.'

She smile. Then her face get serious. 'I hear Lyle's been back. Is that so?'

I hesitate but I sick of lies. 'Yes, a while back. He don't stay though. He is long gone now.' I pour hot water on the coffee grounds. Hand her a cup.

She warm her hands on it, hold it to her. 'I was thinking maybe he brought news of December. Maybe he heard something. Maybe he knows where he is?'

I put my back to her and pour my coffee, try not to give myself away. But then I think why hold back? She gotta right to know. She love him like I do. I turn and face her. 'Yes, he do, he do bring news of December. He…'

Is hard telling someone their darkest fear. I see her eyes light up, like she be expecting good news not bad. Then she see my face. My face be telling the story and there is no stopping it.

142

'What?' She say. 'What is it? Tell me, Aiyana.'

'I am sorry, I am truly sorry, but December, he ain't no more. He is dead, Hannah. That's what Lyle say.'

She cry out. 'No, it's not possible, no, how could he be dead? He's young and fit and he can't be. He can't...' She spill her coffee.

I take the cup from her. Kneel down by her and take her hand. 'It's true. Lyle saw his body on the tracks, fallen from the freight car. It happens a lot. Lyle say the railroad gonna write you but I guess they ain't got round to it yet.'

She is weeping now. I am weeping too. We are holding onto each other. Then she pull away and dry her tears on her handkerchief. Her face is pale with sorrow but there is something else. The thing I see long ago, the time she beat December. The fire of anger blister in Hannah Lutz's eyes.

'Come tomorrow,' she say. 'Bring the book.'

'But daddy say he kill me if he find out you been helping me. Most likely he take it out on you too.'

'I am not afraid. He will not run me out of my home like he did my son. Your daddy and Silas, they are responsible for this, mark my words. I heard it on the river from a reliable source. It wasn't Henry Stamper who drove December out, not that he would have objected. No, his blood is on their hands, Aiyana, and I will never forget and nor should you.'

She take me by the shoulders, grip me tight, look into my eyes. 'Never forget what they do. We will bide our time and I will teach you to read, Aiyana, if it's the very last thing I ever do. And they will pay for this. Believe me.'

I ain't exactly sure what she mean when she say they will pay for what they do. But Hannah Lutz ain't the forgiving kind and if you ask me she is hungry for a reckoning.

Feel her hunger too. See it in the moon. When we be depending on the land for food, and the land been frozen for months we are likely to be hungry. It stand to reason, everyone hungry on the river. Animals too, they down to the bone. But

143

my hunger be different, it ain't for belly food, is for a way out of here. And I been hungry too long. Is time for change, I know it. Hear it in the river song when I am down at Ella's boat. Hear it in Hannah's words. Ain't gonna be hungry forever and that is a fact.

Silas

24

Floyd Weir was a man of powerful desires, the most powerful being his craving to possess everything and everyone round about him. This was the chief reason for his anger when the boy, Lyle, upped and left without a word to him. Nobody did that to Floyd. He was a man to be obeyed. He demanded your loyalty and mostly he got it due in no small measure to his unlimited cruelty and the fear it instilled.

Floyd gave me Aiyana. She was to be my consolation. He said he was mighty sorry about Johnson but the truth was he owed him a debt, and debts between river men could not be overlooked. It led to bad blood, he said, and then he muttered something about a poker game, three kings and a flush. Only I knew different. I knew if he didn't honour his promise Johnson would tell the world what Floyd Weir had done to his own daughter. The river folk are lawless, I grant you, but there is no mistaking their morals and they would have damned him to hell and back for doing such a thing.

It was Floyd who ran Hannah Lutz's boy out of town. He told Henry Stamper that the boy was carrying on with his wife, Crystal, behind his back, calling in at the boat on his way home from work. Stamper was in two minds but Floyd rounded up a posse and there were plenty willing to help, Johnson's acquaintances among them. They belonged to the Klan, or at least some of them did and they liked nothing better than to chase the coloureds off what they deemed to be their territory.

The boy, being mulatto, they were all for lynching him, what with him having been with a white woman, but I was able to persuade Floyd that lynching was not in our interests. Most likely it would bring the law nosing in and we didn't need them poking about. We had the banker and his demise to think of. I said a lynching would bring the law down on us for sure. I told him the guilt from that night still hung heavy with me and that confession was on my mind. For once, Floyd listened to me. So they got their horses and came with their fire and masks, and drove him off the river. At least that way he was still alive and I thought I'd done something for the good.

Floyd instructed me to beat Aiyana. She was used to it, he said, she would expect it. I was to keep her in fear, and it didn't take me long to see why that was how he wanted it. No doubt he was planning on doing to her what he'd done to Hetty, if he hadn't already. For my own part, I was not about to stoop so low as to become a man who beats a woman. Or takes her against her will. I told her there would be no more beatings. All I demanded was that she carry out her wifely duties and abide by my rule of silence. In time, I came to see the silence I imposed as a cruelty every bit as fierce as the belt. I denied her what she deemed most precious in the world, her right to speak and her right to learn to read. I showed no pity. I could have helped her but I did not and I cannot deny that somehow her suffering alleviated mine.

The night Lyle came back that all changed. That night I saw I was no better a man than Floyd Weir and it was time to do something about it. I'd torn the book from her hands, was about to burn it on the stove, when there he was like a spirit standing in the doorway and that dog of his growling at his feet. He looked like a man condemned, like a man who'd been to hell and back. His hair was dishevelled, his clothes were ragged and dirty and hunger stalked him.

Without thinking, I ran out to Floyd's, told him the boy was back and told him how Hannah Lutz was teaching Aiyana to read. I saw his anger flare and I feared what he might do. In that moment, a deep self-loathing came over me and its fire coursed through my body. What had I done? The voice came to me then, a voice I never thought to hear again. It was the voice of my dead wife, Mary. 'Shame on you, Silas. Shame on you.' Her voice rang clear as a bell and it kept repeating in my head. I heard her cough too. The voice, then her cough. There was no peace from it. It wouldn't let up and by the time the night was over I was on my knees praying for her and for God's absolution.

I knew Aiyana was waiting for me to fall asleep. She made some excuse about needing to stay up, so I obliged her, took the bed and pretended to sleep but all the while I watched and waited to see what she was about to do. When she sneaked out I had a good idea where she was going. The second night I followed her to be sure. He was holed up with the dog in the fisherman's cabin by the back of the Bluff. She went there every night until he left. The old woman helped her, providing food and blankets. I knew this but my days of running to Floyd were over. I kept my silence and I prayed that Mary would no longer be ashamed of me.

Aiyana wept for her brother, Lyle, when he left. I saw the change in her. She grieved longer than I would have imagined it possible to grieve for the living, though I'd had a taste of it myself with Mary and again with Hetty. At times she barely moved all day and I could see her spirit was close to breaking. She spent countless nights in the chair by the stove, occasionally crying out in her sleep. I once followed her at dusk to the same hollow place in the woods. And I watched as she wept and kneeled to lay a wreath she'd woven of ivy and winter corn. It was then I began to think of finding a way to set her free.

I heard the voice first, calling from the riverbank and the child crying. Aiyana heard it too and straight away ran out and I followed. It was Hetty, standing on the bank under the willows in an arc of sunshine, and in her arms she cradled a child. My child. My heart swelled large in my chest to see her. She was as beautiful as ever. Johnson was there too, standing back away and my first thought then was whether he knew the child in Hetty's arms was not his. If he did, he didn't show it. Aiyana ran up and took the baby and while the women cooed over him, for he was a boy, Hetty told us they had named him Turner after Johnson's father. Johnson stepped forward and held out his hand to me by way of a greeting. I shook it and looked then for any knowledge of what had passed between Hetty and me but there was no sign. Behind him, Hetty looked up at me and smiled.

Their return was celebrated at Floyd's boat with a fish fry on the riverbank. It was early in the year for being outside, but the sun held and the promise of spring hung in the air. Neighbours, Ada and Pike, joined us and there was a festive air about the afternoon and evening. Even Aiyana smiled and seemed content and engrossed with the child.

When Hetty sat next to me on one of the makeshift wooden benches I felt the brush of her arm on mine. It was the lightest of touches but it sent a shock wave up my arm and through my body, like I'd been stuck with a Texas cattle prod. It fair took my breath from me and I did not dare to look at her for fear of giving myself away. If it was the same for her I could not tell, although I could not help hoping it was.

But something in Hetty had changed. I could see that much. She looked older and somehow far away, like the sun had gone down on her. For the most part, she seemed indifferent to the child and it was Aiyana who nursed him. When the sun caught Hetty's cheek I saw the faint markings of a purple bruise beneath her eye and I wondered then if, like her daddy, Johnson had taken to beating her.

As for the child, he was a handsome boy. I held him in my arms several times that evening and on each occasion I sensed Mary looking down on me and asking me how it was I had forgotten the child I already had. And I saw Eloise in Turner's tiny face and I knew for certain he was mine.

After the fish fry was over and Pike had insisted on taking Hetty and Johnson the mile or so back home, Aiyana rowed across the river with her grandma to see her safely to bed and I made my way back to the boat where I sat by the lamp at the kitchen table and took out my bible.

When Aiyana returned she said nothing, as was our custom.

I said, 'Sit down, why don't you? Sit here, next to me at the table. Would you like me to read to you from the bible, Aiyana?'

I had taken her by surprise. She walked slowly across to the table and sat down next to me. 'Yes, I would, I would like that, Silas,' she said.

So I did: 'In the beginning was the word...'

She put her hand out to stop me. 'Read that again.'

I read it again: 'In the beginning was the word.' I looked up from the bible and saw her smiling. I saw for the first time that I had made her happy.

Aiyana

25

April. Moon of the Winds. *In the beginning was the word.* He read it to me. We come back from the fish fry, everyone there, family, neighbours, Ada and Pike, even the Hartleys, but not Hannah. We celebrating Hetty and Johnson's homecoming with their baby, Turner. When it finish I row grandma across and when I come back Silas tell me to sit down at the table and he will read me from his bible.

Silas say it's from the gospel of John, chapter one, verse one – *In the beginning was the Word, and the Word was with God, and the Word was God.* He read it out and all the time I am thinking hallelujah! I know that is right. I know it all along. That is why I been hungering after learning. The word is everything, it is the beginning of all things. The word is God and the word is in God, like the river is in me, and there's a light gonna shine in my darkness.

I am working hard now to know the word and Hannah says I am almost ready for proper schooling. I am writing words too and speaking them. I don't get it right all the time but I am learning and there is hardly a thing I can't read. My world is alive with words. They are everywhere, falling at me from every place I look, every place I go. Yes, I say to myself, I know that word. Words come tumbling from all the buildings and notices in town, the stores, chemist, the railroad carriages, the side of the biscuit box, mama's Sears catalogue, the book of prayer, words are everywhere and I got the breath for them too. My breath comes easy especially now I know the full stops. Know how to stop and breathe before I carry on.

Hannah, she is a good and patient teacher. She say it's best she keep the books with her so nobody find them. I agree although I ain't sure even if Silas do find them that he go tearing them up and burning them like did before, or that he run and tell daddy. There is a change in him. It's mostly since Hetty came back but even before then I see it. It happen after Lyle's visit. He is different. Like he see my sadness then and he leave me be. He talk to me now and if I ask, sometimes he read to me from his bible.

Hannah teach me in the mornings but I ain't going to her boat on account of maybe Floyd see me. So she teaching me on grandma's boat where we be well out of sight and Floyd never comes. Mostly it's me or mama that go to grandma's boat and mama, she don't say nothing when she's there, she just watch. Reckon she wish she be learning the word too.

Grandma come round to the idea of me learning to read. She say that if that's what it takes to set me free from here then that's what I gotta do. She won't be around much longer anyways, she gotta a journey to go on and she don't like to think of me being here without her to look out for me.

One morning when I am reading to Hannah, mama is sitting there listening and peering over my shoulder at the book and Hannah offer to teach her too. Mama say it's too late, she was never any good at that kind of thing. Hannah say that is nonsense and then grandma, she join in. I never hear her speak to mama like this before.

'No, my daughter, it is not too late. I have been silent for too long. Ojibwe women are brave and strong, we are the ones destined to give life. Remember Bear Woman with a strong heart and mighty courage. She saves the lives of her children. You must look to the spirits and your dreams and to your own life. He has taken the life from you but it is yours to take back.'

Mama don't say nothing at first. We are all silent, thinking what our lives be and how they might be different. After a time mama say to Hannah. 'When Aiyana has learned, then maybe I will begin. Teach her first.'

Grandma seem happy for us to meet on her boat. She know about December. I told her everything and she understands. Told her how Hannah reckon Floyd gonna pay. Grandma say Hannah is right, sooner or later Floyd Weir got to answer for what he do, Silas too. The Great Spirit knows what is in every man's heart.

Although grandma got the mist in the mornings and she forget things and get muddled easy, she still got her wits about her. Only getting slow to move. I tell her she is gonna be around forever but, truth is, when I look at her I see the clouds in her eyes. I see how she grow small and she getting thin like she don't eat properly anymore. She is like the leaf that dry and shrivel up ready to fall. It just take a gust of wind to blow her from the tree.

She don't mind Hannah Lutz any more. Say she is another of Floyd's casualties, more to be pitied, except she got a mighty temper on her. I say I know, I saw her once with December when she beat him and it was worse than what Floyd do. Grandma say maybe he met his match.

I don't ask Hannah about Floyd. I just glad she is teaching me. But I reckon she ain't mixing with him anymore. I reckon he broke her heart, chasing out her only child.

Grandma is making a cradleboard for Hetty to carry Turner in. She make it of wood, got a deer skin mattress for him to rest on. It got leather straps for Hetty's back and a hoop with a dreamcatcher and bells to hang above his head. It got two binding bands she embroider with red and blue flowers and green trailing ivy. He gonna be safe and warm in his cradleboard, providing she hurry. I don't say so but if she don't hurry up, soon he gonna grow too big for it.

I tell grandma I am glad to see Hetty come back but she shake her head and say there gonna be trouble for sure. I ask her what she mean, what kind of trouble, but she don't say nothing, only that she seen it in a dream and it ain't pretty. She making Turner a dreamcatcher for his window as well as the cradleboard but she ain't confident it gonna keep the trouble at bay. It don't make sense to me, how trouble can follow a child like Turner.

He about the prettiest baby I ever saw. Everyone say so. I see him and my cold winter heart melt. It is like I have love again. Ain't the same kind of love a woman have for a man but it is a love that dawn, like the spring on the river. Everything waking up, young born, leaves opening, river got a new life and a new song.

When I ain't at grandma's, I am walking to Hetty and Johnson's house. It's looking mighty fine now, got the veranda finished and got grass all around for when Turner gets to walking and playing. I help Hetty look after Turner, do most everything a mother do for a child bar the feeding and rocking at night. Hetty let me, she is glad of it. Johnson too, he say he gonna build me my very own room so I can live with them and be there day and night. Hetty is tired and her feet all swollen up, been like that since before Turner was born. She say she ain't never known pain like it and she don't ever want to go through that pain again. It take three days before he come into the world, the longest three days of her life. Say daddy's beating don't even come close.

Turner be a fretful child, waking all the time and crying plenty. But he seem good when I come around and Hetty say I am the only one he settle with. When he is in my arms I am happy but then I get to thinking about the child me and December never gonna have and it spoil the happiness. One thing I am grateful of, there ain't no chance of a baby with me and Silas. Everyone keep asking when the wedding gonna happen. When we gonna start a family and why don't I get grandma to make me some special medicine? I smile and say nothing. I know it ain't gonna happen.

Now Hetty's back, Silas got a smile on his face. He stop fussing over his aprons and scrubbing his hands with vinegar. He tell me that he hate that job in the slaughterhouse and he gonna look for something different. He ask me to bring Turner to the boat now the evenings getting warm and light. He is always wanting to see the child, always making a fuss of him. If a stranger come along and see us they most likely think Turner is our child and that's a fact. Though lately, Hetty taken to coming to the boat herself, bringing Turner and sitting with us of an evening. She say Johnson is hammering nails and knocking wood and there ain't no peace. I reckon that just be half the story. She wanting to be near Silas. I see what lies in her heart and in his heart too, ain't no mistaking it. He want Hetty and she want him. They are still in love. But Hetty belong to someone else. She is Johnson's wife and that ain't something can be changed.

Grandma getting worse. I don't meet Hannah on her boat anymore. This last week she don't even know where she is. But I am still hungry to learn, so I go to Hannah's when the men are off at the moonshine shack in the evening. Nights I read. Days I look after grandma.

The mist is spreading to grandma's head. Sometimes she think she is back on the northern plains with her people, sometimes she think granddaddy is still here, she forgets he gone and she start talking to him. Times she ain't sure who mama is or me. She call me *Mitena* and *Migisi* and *First Son*. Mama say those were the names of her babies who died, taken from her before they got to walking. Mama's sisters and mama's brother. Grandma take out her sorrow dolls, made from her own hair. She forget about the cradleboard for Turner.

Even though she is slow and she tired as a fox with three legs, she goes wandering off into the woods and the like and we gotta go looking. One day Pike find her walking on the road to town and he bring her back. Oss Starling bring her back from the ferry too. Hard to see how she get that far but she do. Most times it's me and Floyd go looking and bring her back. He make me go with him. When we are out searching I don't speak even though he try to be soft on me. I give him the look that say, don't you touch me. I swear, he ever try and touch me again I gonna kill him. Trouble is, he the kind of man got to take his anger out on someone, most likely he'll be starting on the twins soon. But he don't seem to get angered with grandma, not like he do with most people and that is a blessing. Got me a notion he just might be afraid of her and the spirits she got around her. He say by his reckoning she ain't got long for this world and I better prepare myself.

I am on grandma's boat, washing her deck, when I see Silas and Hetty across the water on the riverbank. He is coming home from work and she is there to meet him. It's like he teasing her about something and then she laughing and acting all coy. I don't hear what they say but I see it boiling up between them, like the spring flood, just a matter of time. She pass Turner to him and I see the way he look down on the child in his arms. He is seeing what I see, clear as spring water. Ain't no way Turner is Johnson's child and that is a fact.

I ain't jealous. I am smiling inside. Silas has taken his eye off me for sure and soon it's gonna be my chance to get away. Except there is no way I can leave Grandma. I need to be here at the end to make sure her spirit go to the right place. I know she needs me. I know this is something I gotta do.

26

I am up before the sun. Mist lie like frost on the water. Smoke-river, snake-river, river of cloud and breath, wear the dawn like a mask. I hear the wood duck calling, watch the swan come and dip her feather neck, see the doe and fawn drink at the water's edge. The river be life to all and soon its path be my path and its water quench my thirst.

When Silas leave for the slaughter house, I make coffee and sit at the table and think of my reading. Hannah say I gotta keep practising now. I go to the bedroom to fetch Tom Sawyer and the new Sears catalogue and that's when I see Silas's bible, on top of the cottonwood chest. For once it ain't locked away. I pick it up, think I might read it for myself, and I take it to the kitchen table, lay it down and open it up.

The front page is a clean page but there is writing on it in blue ink. I read what it say. 'To our daughter Mary, on the occasion of her...' I ain't sure about the last word *betrothal*. It puzzling me, so I copy it down on a scrap of paper and put it in my pocket to show Hannah. It's got a date underneath, say *In The Year of Our Lord 1929*. Seems like it don't belong to Silas after all, unless he be given it. I wonder who Mary is. It don't feel right to be reading her bible so I close it and put it back where I find it and set about my chores before I row across the river to grandma's.

The sun is low in the sky and the swifts chasing up and down river when Silas return from work. He take his apron off, go outside and wash up. He sit at the table to eat his meal and I sit opposite.

I already made up my mind to ask him about Mary and the bible, so I come out with it straight. 'Who is Mary, Silas?'

He stop eating. Look up from his plate, it's like he see the dead in the doorway but he say nothing.

'I'm asking about Mary,' I say.

'I don't know who you mean.'

I ain't about to let on that I am reading now and that I read his bible on the kitchen table, so I say, 'Must be someone, else why you calling her name out when you asleep. It is always Mary you call for.'

'Mary?'

'Mary.' I look him straight in the eyes.

He put down his fork, bow his head and in a quiet voice he say, 'Mary was my wife, Aiyana.'

I fall back in my chair. 'Your wife, Mary was your wife? How can that be? Is she still your wife?'

'No, she is no longer my wife. Mary died in the dust storms, from pneumonia. The dust choked her.'

'God have mercy,' I gasp. I reach my hand out to his across the table. Our fingertips touch. 'I am sorry. Truly, it is a terrible thing. Did you love her very much, Silas?'

'I loved her, yes.'

'And children?' I ask, thinking that ain't possible, surely he ain't leaving a child behind. Maybe he have a child and it die too. Maybe more than one.

He nod. Pull his hand away and rest his head on it.

'How many? Boy, girl?'

'One. I have one child, a girl. She is called Eloise.'

'You got a child. Is she alive or...is she gone? Did she die with your wife?'

'No, she's alive somewhere, only I'm not exactly sure where she is right now.'

'You got a living child, Silas, and you don't know where she be, you don't even know about your own child, your own flesh and blood?' As I say this I feel my heart beat fast. I can't help thinking of my daddy, wherever he be.

'I left her with the neighbours. Went out West in search of work. It was for all our benefit, but then we lost touch and...'

'You got a child you left behind, she out there somewhere and you ain't out there looking for her? You just spending your time here on the river. Well, maybe that's because you got another child.'

He sit back in his seat like he take a punch to the chest. 'I don't know what you mean, Aiyana.'

'I ain't stupid, Silas, I see how he looks like you. Turner is your boy and there is no mistaking it. Don't deny it, Silas. I am sick of secrets and lies. I see how it is with you and Hetty, how it's always been. Trouble is, Johnson gonna see soon enough and then there be a whole heap of trouble.'

Silas don't deny it, he just bow his head and look down at the half-eaten food on his plate. Then he push the plate hard across the table and it fall and clatter on the boards. He stand up, fetch his coat and go outside.

Ain't long before I hear Floyd's voice calling him and they go off to drink at Elmer Glass's shack in the woods. But no matter how much moonshine he gonna drink, I see he cannot escape his fate. It run like the river, ain't no stopping it and he is caught up in the ebb and flow, whichever way he turn he is going under. Maybe he deserve it. If he helped Floyd run December out of town then he do deserve it. Truth is we don't always get what we deserve but when that happens we gotta act, when we be at the mercy of the river we gotta swim against the flow with all our will.

Dusk and the air turn blue. I walk along the bank to mama's boat. Wind in the grass, wild turkey on the path. Frogs start up their croaking and smoke hang over the Bluff, from the burning of the prairie, like it do every spring. There still be

160

folks out there trying to coax a living from the land. When I reach the boat I whistle and call to mama, 'Coming down. Come to look at my photograph.'

She fetch the photograph for me. I hold it up to the lamp and look at myself. But it ain't just me I am seeing. I am thinking about him, my daddy, the man who left me, wonder if I look like him. Think soon I gotta ask mama and she gotta tell me. She owe me that. Then I take the pencil I been carrying from my pocket and write my name on the back in big, clear letters. I see those red sails coming on and Ella P. Fry tall and still as a statue. I smile and wonder if she be on her way back.

I give the photograph back to mama and she put it away again for safe keeping. 'Ada's been looking for you, Aiyana, she was here this morning. She didn't say what it was, just said to be sure and tell you to call on her.'

'I think it's too late for calling now. It's past time to row across to grandma and put her to bed. I'll call on Ada tomorrow.'

'I'll come with you to your grandma's,' mama say. 'The twins are asleep and there's nothing spoiling here.'

We go out together up the gangplank, onto the bank where the bats circling overhead. I haul up the row boat and hold it for mama. She step in and sit down. I climb in after her and push off with my oar. Red sky on the skin of still water. We are shadows on the fiery mirror, half-seen, we are a thing of spirit and dream. I am thinking I might row and row into the falling sun. Take me and mama out of this place, way down to the wide ocean. We might catch a boat there like Hannah Lutz and her mama, all that time ago. We might travel to a new land.

Grandma's boat is unusual quiet. She ain't in the kitchen.

'Must be in bed already.' And so she is. She is on her bed of furs but she ain't dressed for sleeping. She dressed like she is going somewhere special, like she is going back to her people. Got her tunic with painted flowers and beads on, made of hide, got fringe and a belt that belonged to her mama. She's put her leggings on too and her moccasins. When mama ask her why she dressed up like that she say she's getting ready, she's tired and she gonna sleep before her long journey.

I tell mama I will stay here and sleep beside her.

Our sleep is peaceful. Come morning, I rise early, make grandma tea and tell her I got somewhere I gotta go but I will be back before long. She seem happy just to lie, got her sorrow dolls and her dreamcatchers by her side.

27

I row across the river to Ada's. She is already out, planting her tomatoes. When she see me she look around like she making sure nobody is watching and then she say, 'Got something for you, Aiyana, it came yesterday. Come inside now.'

Pike and Ada's boat is full to overflowing with everything she need for her tomato growing, like crates and bags of fertilizer and canes and string and the like. There is barely room to walk to the table. She has to clear a chair for me to sit down.

'Been keeping it here for safekeeping.' She pick up an old tea caddy and screw off the lid. It takes all her strength to loosen it. Then she pull out a letter, got a postage stamp and all and my name written on it. 'The post delivered it here. It's got mine and Pike's address you see. I guess he was mindful of what he was doing. Your brother that is. Lyle's name is right here on the back. See, look.' She turn it over and point.

I see his name and under it his address, it is New Orleans. I take it from her and thank her for keeping it.

'Do you want me to read it to you? See what he's got to say for himself?'

'Thank you, but that won't be necessary,' I reply.

I take off to the hollow place where no one gonna see me. I am running through the cottonwoods til I get there. Sit down, steady my hand and open Lyle's letter. It is short, a page long and no more. I read every last word that he write.

Dear Aiyana

I hope you are well. I am doing just fine here in New Orleans. I am in lodgings with a good woman, Mrs D. Miller in Canal Street at number 54. I have a job in the docks loading cotton.

I write to tell you that I will be leaving soon, going west into Louisiana where I have been promised work and a place to live on a sweet potato farm by a gentleman, name of Daniel LaSalle. I informed Mr LaSalle that I was expecting you to join me soon and he said that my sister would be welcome. There is work for you too. He is a good man, Aiyana, and we can have a good life there I am sure.

I leave on the twenty eighth day of May. If you come by that date then we can set out together. It will take you five, maybe six days to reach New Orleans by boat, it is the safest way. Ask Oss Starling and he will help you get passage on a boat coming down river. You can depend on him. Come quickly, Aiyana, I am waiting. Castor is waiting too.

Your loving brother
Lyle.
May 4th

I fold his letter up and push it deep into my pocket. I go back past Ada's and I ask her what the date be now. She say it is the sixteenth day of May. When I get back to the boat I count it all out in mussel shells. Reckon I got just twelve days, minus the six it will take me to get there. In six days I must be gone from here.

There just one thing. That be grandma. I ain't sure about leaving her, not when she seems so small and so far away. But then I think of what she say about Bear Woman and I know I must be strong like her.

May. Blossom Moon. Wild plum in flower. White blossom blow on the breeze, fall to skin on the water and let the river carry it away. Soon it will be me, I will be the white petal heading downstream to where I never been before and Lyle waiting. Since his letter come I am thinking of nothing else. I am only thinking of one thing, and that is when? But before I go, I gotta to speak with mama.

She sitting out in the old cane chair that rock, under the washing line strung across the deck, hidden by the sheets blowing in the wind. I call out to her. Then I sneak under the washing and come next to her, sit down on the stool. Ain't no easy way to do this and time running out so I say it straight out, 'Mama, there's something I need to ask you.'

'Ask away child.'

'Is about daddy.' I wait. 'Thing is, I know Floyd ain't my daddy. My daddy someone else, ain't he mama?'

She don't look directly at me but stare ahead at the trees and the water. 'I can't deny it. It's true. Floyd ain't your daddy. I was fixing on telling you, I just never seemed to find the right time. I'm sorry, Aiyana, I should have told you long ago.'

I am holding my breath, waiting for her to go on.

'Your daddy was a fine man, Aiyana, wouldn't hurt a fly. He was nothing like Floyd. Worked for the railroad company, came and went with them and I don't rightly know where he is now. I don't know nothing about him above his name and that he was the sweetest, kindest man I ever knew. Call him Davy Gillion, out of Illinois. Your grandma said he had Cherokee blood but that was just a fanciful notion she dreamed up.' She get up from the cane chair. 'I got something of his for you. Been keeping it this long while.' She step off the deck and into the kitchen.

I follow mama inside. She go into the bedroom and over to the Angel Chest, kneel down and she lift its lid. I see the bible there, the one I always wanted. It is not of my family. I know that now. She put her hands in under the clothes and linen and feel around like she know exactly what she is looking for. Then she bring it up. It's the smallest thing, tucked in the end of a stocking that have a knot in it. 'Here,' she say and she hand it to me. 'He wasn't here above three months and he didn't know I was with child when he left. But he gave me these. Reckon they must be worth something. All these years with no money, the times we've been hungry but I never once thought of selling them. I've been keeping them for you, Aiyana. This is all I have of him to give you.'

I take the stocking from mama and untie the knot. I put my hand inside and bring up two white pearls. I lay them in the palm of my hand, silver raindrops hanging on the willow, white berries of the mistletoe, tears of the river, the most precious gift I ever have.

Grandma sit on her bed of furs. She ain't lying down any more. Her cheeks be rosy and she lost that far off look. I sit next to her, sun floating in, falling on my knees, dust spinning in the air.

'What is it, Wild Plum? You are different. Your thoughts are far off.'

'It's Lyle,' I say. 'He write to me from New Orleans. He is living in lodgings, got a job loading cotton on the docks but he's fixing to go west to Louisiana. Say there be work there for both of us. Say I should come.'

Grandma puts her tea down. She is listening hard. 'I see.'

'He met a gentleman and he got work on his sweet potato farm. It's all the rage, Ada say so, sweet potato is the vegetable of the future.'

Grandma smile. 'Well, that's something, sweet potato indeed. But how will you get there, child?'

'Got to get me a boat. Lyle say if I go see Oss Starling he will help find one. Trouble is, I only got six days before I gotta to be gone, waste two already, so it have to be soon.'

'Well, what are you waiting for, child? You must fly like the eagle. It is your time. The wild plum is in blossom so what better time can there be for you to set out? Travelling is something we Ojibwe women understand. Besides, I will be gone myself any day now when I am fully strong and ready. I have my own journey to make. Soon, the first strawberries will ripen and the wild rice will be ready to harvest. Soon, I will be back with my people to harvest with them, as my mother and her mother before her. I am returning to my clan. It is time for both of us to leave.'

'You are going north, to the Lakes? But, grandma, that is a long journey.'

'No journey is long that is worth making. This will be the worthiest and happiest journey I have yet to make. Yours will be likewise.'

'Will your clan be waiting?'

'They will be waiting for me as Lyle is waiting for you. Remember we are Crane. This is our kinship. The crane stands in the water and watches the world around her and she knows how to live with people not her own. This is your gift. You are Crane. Take your gift with you, Wild Plum, and go with my blessings.'

I hear what she say but I am still thinking it will be impossible to leave her. She is the one person I can never leave.

'I know what you are thinking but we will meet again, my child, where Gichi-Manidoo is waiting, beyond the path of the winds, at the edge of the world, among the stars. Make haste now. Go to Mr Starling, he is a good man and take this with you, it will keep you from harm. When you come back I will be gone.'

She presses snakeroot in my palm and then a deerskin purse that she sewed herself, small enough to fit in my pocket.

'It has dollars in,' she say. 'You will need dollars, Wild Plum. Every journey has its necessities and the traveller must be prepared.'

She stand on the deck in the sun and wave me goodbye. She watch until I am out of sight. I know because I look back every turn and she is still there like a shadow in the light. And I look hard, I take a photograph in my mind like I do, in case this be my very last sight of grandma.

28

I make my way through the chokecherry bushes and trees upstream to where Oss Starling keep the ferry. When I get to the crossing place he is already on the other side at the loading bay. I wait for him bringing the ferry boat back. See he got two passengers, so I make myself scarce, hiding away until he docks and they climb off and disappear. I come out of my hiding place then and see Oss sitting on his old stone chewing grass. When he see me walk up he takes the grass out of his mouth.

'Well now, Missy, and what can I do for you this bright morning? You planning on taking another trip across river?'

'Not exactly,' I say.

'Not exactly, now what does that mean, not exactly?'

'It's hard to say. It's a kind of secret.'

'Well now, I guess if it's a secret you won't be telling me, unless that is you are hoping I might be good at keeping secrets?'

'I think I am hoping that you be good at secrets because if my daddy finds out, or if Silas finds out, then I will probably be in a whole heap of trouble. I ain't wanting to lie to you, Mr Starling. You been kind to me and I reckon you deserve better. So if it be impossible for you to keep my secret, given my daddy be Floyd Weir, then I understand and I'll be on my way.'

He look at me hard. Put the grass back in his mouth and chew a while. Take it out and say, 'Well now, I gotta be honest here, Floyd Weir never was my most favourite person in the world. Not that I'm saying anything against him directly, but he ain't no special friend of mine. So if I can help you I will, Missy, and I'll be glad of it.'

I think of what grandma say about how he is a good man, how I know this myself. Think I ain't got no choice but to trust him. 'My brother Lyle sent me. He say you might help me.'

'Your brother, Lyle? Well now, last I hear he down on the Delta working in the docks. Least that's what a little passing bird told me.'

'He is but he planning on going to work on a Louisiana farm and I figuring on joining him but I need me a passage down river and there ain't much time now. I gotta be gone in less than four days. You are the one who knows what boats coming and going that I might get a passage on.'

'Well now, I reckon you've come to the right place, Missy. Louisiana, that's some journey, sounds to me like the pair of you ain't figuring on coming back. Let me think a while. You just missed the Delta Queen, she passed by yesterday. There are the fishery boats of course but I reckon it's gonna be mighty hard, if not impossible, for a young woman such as yourself to get on board one of them. Logging boats, no chance. Now let me think. Hmm. Reckon the only one will be The Verity. She ain't against picking up the odd passenger, as long as you got dollars, ain't no free rides I'm afraid. You got dollars?'

'I got dollars.'

'Good. Well she coming by tomorrow about six in the evening. Reckon you can make it for tomorrow. Ain't too short notice and all?'

'I can make it.'

'Best you be here early so I can take you across beforehand. Stay there while it dock and fix it up for you. How does that sound, now? And while I am at it, best you don't come with much in the way of luggage, no cases, no baggage. You'd be surprised who see what goes on, on this here riverbank. If you don't want people being suspicious, fetching your daddy and the like, come as empty handed as you can.'

'I will. Got precious little to bring with me anyways so that sound just fine. Can't thank you enough, Mr Starling.'

'Well, no thanks needed. Just you be here on time and everything gonna work out fine. Before you know it, you be away with that brother of yours high tailing it off down to Louisiana.'

Lyle was right. Oss was the man to go to. My heart is singing with the river as I make my way back to grandma's yellow boat. Mama is there. She standing on the deck and she looking like she growing up out the reeds, just like the boat always do. She call when she see me. 'Aiyana, where've you been? I've been calling and calling for you.'

'Took a walk.' I try to sound like I do most days, when everything is ordinary, when I am not the river about to overspill its banks. Try not to sound like I am a bird waiting to fly the nest, nervous as a baby chick looking down and flapping its wings. 'Been looking for wild strawberries. I was thinking grandma might like some.'

'Surely you know it's too early for strawberries. Never mind. Grandma's not here. I thought I'd come across and here she'd be lying in her bed and then when she wasn't, I thought she must be with you. Surely she don't have the strength to go off on her own.'

I am alongside the boat now and I see the worried look on mama's face. 'She do, she do have strength. Why, this morning she sitting up eating your biscuits and drinking berry tea. She say she building up her strength, she is going on a journey, mama, to her clan, to her people from the north.'

'Nonsense, she ain't got the legs for a journey like that. It's hundreds of miles. She'll be off somewhere wandering in the woods, waiting for someone to go looking and fetch her home.'

'I think she mean it, mama, what she say and all, she wanting to go and harvest the wild rice. She say it's her time and no journey is too long if it worth making.'

'Well, we'll see. Reckon when Floyd get home he'll be out looking for her, maybe he'll take Silas with him. Will you tell Silas when he comes in from work?'

'I'll tell him mama, soon as he gets back.'

We get in the boat and row back across the water. I look around me, drink it in, make another photograph in my mind, something to keep, soon I be gone from here. I gonna miss the river for sure but it live in me. Always. No matter how far I go.

Silas and Floyd are out looking for grandma. By my reckoning she is long gone and they ain't gonna find her even if they looking for thirteen moons. I got my things packed: my snakeskin root, my dollar purse, *The Adventures of Tom Sawyer* and my pearls tied in mama's stocking. Put them in a flour sack bag so it look like I'm gonna get goods from the Store, or fish, or wild roots. I ain't leaving my book behind. Gotta have it when I get to New Orleans. Lyle gonna be mighty surprised when I open it and read him some.

I wish I could tell mama that I am going but I'm afraid that if I tell her, Floyd gonna find out. He gonna see she ain't right, he will know something is up. So I keep quiet. I don't ask her for my photograph even though I want it bad. Think when I get to Louisiana I just have to get me another photograph. Mama can keep the one she got so she still have something of me with her. Once I am safe with Lyle I will write to her for sure.

I go out on deck and sit a while. Listen for Silas and Floyd coming back. Watch the white owls float above the water and the fingernail moon rise above the black trees. I pray for tomorrow, for it to come as soon as is possible, for nothing to stop me now. When all the light is gone and the stars show their face I go back inside, slip into my bed and tell the night to hurry its way to morning.

I wake in the darkness, when Silas come into the bedroom. He stand by the bed and tell me they don't find grandma. His voice is thick in his throat and I smell the moonshine on his breath. Then he turn away and go back to his bed on the boards and I spend the rest of the night drifting in and out of sleep.

It is just before dawn when I hear them. They come as the birds are starting up and it ain't just one motor, it's three, cracking the silence, pulling up on the dirt track running along the bank, brakes squeal in the dust. I wonder who can be up this early, in this much of a hurry and where they be going, when the next thing I hear be the boots heavy on the plank.

They coming to us and no mistake. The boat shift and complain under their weight as they step on deck. I am already up and out of bed, pulling my coat around my nightgown just as the knocking start. It is a fierce sound.

'Open up now,' bark the voice outside and it ain't a friendly voice. It's an angry voice insisting on getting its way. It be a voice in a hurry, a voice to be obeyed.

I open the door and see the silver badges and the lapels, the guns out of the holsters. Sheriff Harper is there. I know him straight away, we all know him, he is practically one of us, anything wrong on the river and he always the one to come. He got two deputies with him, look like he is expecting trouble.

'Aiyana,' he nod at me. 'I'm looking for Silas, Aiyana, he here?'

'Yes. He's sleeping. Why? What happened? Is it grandma, has something happened to her?'

'No. But I'll be needing to speak with him now. Be taking Silas in, back with us, so I reckon it's best if we come in and wake him while you go fetch his boots and coat.'

The deputies push past me, touching their hats as they go, then kick open the bedroom door.

'He ain't in there. He is here.' I point to the bed on the boards

Silas is already awake and sitting up. I fetch his coat from the hook and his boots from where he usually leave them by the stove. When I pick them up I see they leave a print on the floor. It is made in blood.

They tell Silas to get dressed. 'Hurry now,' say Sheriff Harper, 'we're taking you in.'

Silas stands in the kitchen, owl face and white, he got his trousers and shirt on. They pull his hands behind his back and put the cuffs on him.

'What is it? What's he done? He's been here asleep, can't be anything.' But then I think of the print on the floor, it is blood for sure. How do I know what Silas might do, or what he is capable of?

'We're taking him in now for questioning, Aiyana. Why don't you sit yourself down there.' He points to the table. 'Take him away, boys.' The deputies lead Silas away, head hanging low.

'What is it, Sheriff? What's he done? Please I gotta right to know.'

'He's wanted in connection with the murder of Johnson Crawford.'

'The murder of Johnson? Hetty's Johnson? He's dead? It ain't possible.' I hold on to the back of the chair and steady my breath.

'I'm afraid so, Aiyana. Johnson's dead. Died in the County Hospital, pronounced dead on arrival as a matter of fact. Three minutes past midnight. Died of a knife wound.'

'But Silas, he don't carry a knife.'

'Well now, that's not what I hear. But we'll see when we get to questioning him and all. Thing is we got witnesses. Happen up at Elmer Glass's place.'

I lower myself into the chair. Johnson, Johnson is dead and Silas killed him. I cannot believe what Sheriff Harper say, must be some kind of mistake but then why is he here at my table before morning and why have they taken Silas down to the jailhouse if it ain't true?

'I'm mighty sorry, Aiyana. Sorry about Johnson, and sorry about this. I'm just doing my job. I hope you can see that. Perhaps you can come down to the jail later, bring him something to eat and a change of clothes.'

I nod. I cannot speak.

Sheriff Harper's boots echo on the morning as he take his leave.

Silas

29

We went to look for the Ojibwe grandmother but she was nowhere to be found. Floyd said she'd come home soon enough and he was sick of looking for the old woman. Said he was tired of her tricks. It didn't seem as if it were a trick to me or as if she'd gone walkabout like all the other times. One of the Hartley boys said he'd seen her heading north-west up river. Floyd said good riddance, she was getting to be a liability and the best thing we could do was head off for Elmer's. He seemed far from happy though. Something was niggling at Floyd Weir, something was paining him like a splinter lodged deep under the skin. Something wasn't right in his world and you knew about it just by looking at him.

I figured that more than likely it was Hannah Lutz. Hannah Lutz was the splinter under Floyd's skin and no mistake. Until recent times, more often than not, he called in to see her on his way to Elmer's. He would tell me to wait for him on the bank side by the twisted willow. He was rarely more than five minutes but he always came out smiling and whistling. She had the gift of putting Floyd in a good mood. Most evenings on our way back I would leave him there and he would disappear into her boat. It was a fact of life on the river and I reckon there was hardly a person didn't know about Floyd Weir and Hannah Lutz.

But lately things had changed. He'd stopped calling in, stopped making for her boat on his way home except for the evening Johnson was killed. On our way to Elmer's he stopped by the willow and told me to wait. He said he had a gift for Hannah. It was a sweetener, he said, women could not resist a gift, and he pulled a box from his pocket, opened it and showed me the silver bracelet, sat on a blue cushion. Said he'd bought it from a banker he'd taken out fishing. Told me it cost him the best part of the dollars he'd made on that trip and I didn't doubt it.

I couldn't help but hear the raised voices, hers above his and he came out looking less than pleased with himself. 'Well, at least she didn't throw it in the river,' he said and I wondered then how his mind worked. Surely any man with sense could see that running a woman's only child out of town was not the way to her heart. Surely he knew he had a price to pay and it was not something a piece of jewellery would buy. But then, as was so often the case with Floyd, he seemed blind to the consequences of his own actions and I supposed on reflection I was not in a place to criticise him considering my own shortcomings.

'She'll soften up, you see,' he said as we continued walking. 'Woman on her own like that, who else has she got? It's just a matter of time and I ain't in a hurry.' But he didn't convince me and how much he believed in it himself, I could not tell.

Floyd was a big drinker and that night was no exception. He drank heavily and for the most part alone. He sat at a table in the corner of the room where it was darkest and spoke to no one. The shack had two rooms separated by a makeshift partition, out back the room was used for the purpose of playing poker. Johnson was out there with three or four others playing stud and later on Floyd got up from his seat and went out there to join them.

I stood watching and talking to Oss Starling the ferryman. Poker was not a game I knew or wanted to know. Moonshine had loosened my tongue and I told Oss how I badly needed to get out of the slaughterhouse. How blood was infecting my dreams. It was a brutal environment and to my way of thinking it brutalised the men who worked in it. Oss agreed with me, said he'd had a taste of it once, a long time back, said he thought sometimes folks gotta find a way to better themselves. The river wasn't everything, sometimes it took a hold of you and you had to shake yourself up and move on. I thought it strange talk for a man who had lived on the river his whole life and for whom the river was his livelihood. But I had no time to ask him more about his thinking because that's when the shouting started.

I looked up to see Floyd pick up the table and throw it across the room, everything scattering from it to the floor – cards, drinks, cigarettes. Then in an instant he was at Johnson's throat and I saw him take out his hunting knife. I threw myself at him, did my best to wrestle the knife from him but he had an iron grip. Floyd had the strength of the bear at the kill and no man was going to take his knife from him that night. Several of us tried to pull him back, tell him to take it easy, but then before we knew it the knife was in Johnson's neck and the next thing he was on the floor, blood pooling around him, pumping from his body. I have never in all my days seen so much blood flow from a man and there be no stopping it. Johnson emptied out right there in front of us and Floyd stood over him and watched like it was happening to someone else.

They put Johnson in the back of Elmer's truck and took him to the hospital but if you ask me it was a fruitless journey. Any man with any sense could see that Johnson was already dead.

I told Floyd he needed to get out of there and he needed to clean up. He didn't argue, just followed me. He washed the blood from his hands in the river. But his clothes were soaked in it. I told him to get rid of the knife but it was as if he didn't hear me. He stumbled back up the bank and along the path to the twisted willow and without a word to me, he disappeared down into Hannah Lutz's boat. I left him there and came home.

What had caused Floyd to take his knife to Johnson was a mystery. To my way of thinking Johnson had done nothing to anger Floyd that night but I had not been at the card table. Besides, I had seen Floyd take out his knife once before. I knew what little provocation he needed.

When we got to the Sheriff's office, they took me out back into the jailhouse and cuffed me to a chair. They charged me there and then with Johnson's murder, said they had witnesses, more than one, and Floyd Weir among them. Witnesses who were prepared to swear that I had taken my knife to Johnson's throat. They said it was pointless me protesting, after all didn't everyone roundabout know that I wanted Johnson's wife. They said the whole riverbank knew about me and Hetty. I denied it of course but it was like howling into the wind and trying to stop the dust. They asked me what I had done with the knife. I told them it wasn't me, it wasn't my knife. They took my boots and belt and locked me in the cell.

Aiyana

30

Hetty is the tree that lost its roots, torn up in the wind. Without Johnson all Hetty's strength is gone. She cries and cries and there ain't no consoling her. It seem as if the whole river arrive on mama and daddy's boat, neighbours and the like, Johnson's family. All come to pay their respects. All come to grieve. Hetty don't want to see no one. Turner cling to me and I do my best to calm him. Floyd has gone duck shooting, say he have no choice, the men come down from the city for their leisure and it's his business to take them out. Grandma is nowhere to be seen. Part of me is wishing she be here like she always is but then I get to thinking she don't need no more sorrow in her life. She's got her chosen journey to make like I got mine, only now a great, wide boulder roll down from the mountain and block my path.

Everyone talking about Silas and how guilty he is. Even Hetty. I sit out on deck with Turner, rock him to sleep. Feel the dollars in the deerskin purse that I put in my pocket. My dollars be safe but to what purpose? I ain't buying my passage out of here at six o'clock tonight on The Verity. Not now. It just ain't gonna happen.

Sheriff Hartley comes by past noon, gives his condolences to Hetty and tells me I need to come with him because they after searching our boat. I hand Turner over to mama and follow the Sheriff. When we get there he say I need to bring food and a change of clothes to the jailhouse for Silas. He say gather it now and he gonna take me back in the Sheriff's car.

While they be searching, I find cornbread and dried fish and a piece of smoked meat for Silas, get out his Sunday clothes, they the only clothes he got besides what he's wearing and his work aprons. I find his bible under the bed in the chest.

When I am sure they ain't looking, I fetch my flour sack bag with *The Adventures of Tom Sawyer* and my pearls and my snakeskin root, and wait for the Sheriff. As we are leaving I go to put on my coat.

'You won't be needing a coat,' Sheriff Harper say, 'it's as warm as summer on the river, why the corn will be turning from green before we know it.' I put my coat back on the hook.

At the jailhouse I follow Sheriff Harper into the narrow passage at the back of his office. It smell of men, it smell of stale blood and crows' wings. He's got a bunch of keys, big as a lantern. He rattle them along the iron bars in front of the cells til we get to Silas.

Silas is sat in his cell on a mattress on the floor. It got rips and tears, is stained yellow, like a hundred men who never washed slept on it. He looks up. He is a sorry sight but he pleased to see me, I can tell.

The Sheriff fetch me a wooden chair and put it inside the cell. I sit down and he say, 'You be alright here?' I nod. 'OK now, Aiyana, you got fifteen minutes or thereabouts. You need me, you holler. I'll just be in the office there.'

I nod. He leave then and lock me in the cell with Silas.

I give him the bible and the parcel of food and clothes. He ain't hungry, he just thank me and he put the food and clothes to one side but he hold on tight to the bible.

'I know what you are thinking,' he say, 'but it ain't true. I swear it ain't.'

'How do you know what I am thinking?'

'You are thinking you are not surprised. That I am in love with your sister, Hetty, and always have been. That is true,

183

Aiyana. I love her and Turner is my son. I won't deny it. But I did not kill Johnson and I swear this is the truth. I swear here on this book.' He hold the bible up in his hand. 'I swear on Mary's bible, I did not, so help me God, kill Johnson Crawford. Please, believe me.' He look to see what is in my eyes. 'I am sorry for everything I have done to you, Aiyana. I am truly sorry and I ask if you can find it in your heart to forgive me?'

He put his head in his hands then, like a man condemned, and I see a tear fall from his eye to the mattress and despite everything, despite all the lies and cheating, I believe him. It is as if they are swept away and in my heart I believe Silas is telling me the truth.

'I believe you,' I say. 'But if you didn't kill him then who did and where is the knife?'

He turns his head away. His breathing is hard. Like the words won't come, like the river flood his lungs.

'Who, Silas? Tell me this much?'

He turns back to me. 'Your daddy, Aiyana. Floyd killed Johnson and that is not a word of a lie. And as far as the knife is concerned then I think Hannah Lutz will know something of that. He went to her boat when we left Elmer's. Everyone who was there that night knows it was Floyd, that he did it with his hunting knife. Ask Oss Starling, though I imagine like all the others he will not have the courage to speak out.'

'But surely they ain't gonna let an innocent man hang, Silas?'

'No? Think, Aiyana. Floyd's got this place tied up, everyone at his beck and call, doing as he says. Jump when he say jump, like when he run December out of town. I tried to stop him, believe me but it was no use. Can't you see that standing against Floyd is too big a risk? What if no one else dares and you are just one man on your own? What then? Nobody wants to be that man so they turn the other way and they let Floyd carry on doing what he does best, using up all the people around him, bringing misery and terror even to his own kin, and then wasting the land and the river too.'

I cannot deny what Silas says. Every word he say about Floyd is true and the rage in my heart for him spills over. 'I will tell them and they are gonna believe me if I tell on my own father. No one do that if it ain't true.'

'No. You must not do that Aiyana. Believe me. Listen to me, please. Most likely Floyd already paid off the Sheriff. Did you think of that?'

'Sheriff Harper?'

'Every man has his price, Aiyana. It is too late, the most I can do is find a lawyer and claim self-defence, say Johnson had a knife too and he threatened me. They're bringing a lawyer for me in the morning, they will allow me that much at least.'

'Then I will go and see the lawyer on your behalf. Maybe I can put him right about a thing or two. Maybe Hetty can put him right about what daddy do to her and I don't just mean the beatings.'

'No, Aiyana.' He shake his head. 'It won't work. They won't believe you. They will say you are making it all up. But there is something you can do, there are two things I ask you to do for me. Please. Although it's more than I deserve I know.' Silas kneeling on his mattress now, like he is in prayer

'What is it, Silas?'

'I want you to go, Aiyana. I want you to leave this godforsaken river and get away from him forever. It is your only chance and no one deserves that chance more. You cannot give a thought to the others now. Never mind Hetty and Turner, they will survive, but you, if you stay here you will die. He will take the life from you. He will own you forever and you will never be free. Go and find Lyle, find December, learn to read, Aiyana. I know you've started learning, I know that much and I know you've got a future ahead of you but you will only see that future if you escape this place. Believe me.'

185

'I do.' I don't tell him then that December is dead. Reckon he has guilt enough to bear. 'And the second thing?'

'This,' he say and he place a piece of paper in my hand, folded so small it fit in the cuff of his sleeve. 'Take this, it is the address of Otto and Greta's farm. It is my belief that one day they will return with my daughter, Eloise. When you can, I want you to write to them and to Eloise. Tell them if you will that I was not all bad, just that I lost my way.

Now go. Do not go back to the boat. Strike out along the river. It is growing dark already and no one will find you that way. God be with you, Aiyana,' he say and then he take my hand and he kiss it and it be a tender thing, the most respectful thing he ever do.

Nightfall. The Verity long gone without me. I stand by the twisted willow and think of December. He is living in my heart still. I tell him what I am going to do and I ask him to come with me and watch over me.

Hannah look surprised to see me. 'Aiyana. I heard what happened. How is Hetty? How is...'

I interrupt. I have little time now. Already mama and Hetty will be wondering where I am and Floyd too if he is back from fishing. 'I need your help, Hannah, and Silas he need your help too.' She look flustered, like she been caught doing something she shouldn't. 'I know Floyd was here last night, after he killed Johnson. I know he came here with his clothes all bloody and his hunting knife.'

She is about to deny it. I look up at the photograph of her mama and papa looking down on us. She follow my eyes.

'It is true,' she say. 'He was here.'

'He bring his knife?'

She nod.

'You still got it? You hiding it? After all you say about how he gonna pay for what he did to December. How you were never gonna forget and neither should I.'

186

She don't answer.

'Silas, he is sitting up in the jailhouse in a cell right now, charged with something he did not do. He is not guilty, Hannah, and this is your chance to make Floyd pay and save an innocent man. It was Floyd who ran December off the river and no mistake. Silas have nothing to do with it. Think of December, Hannah. Think of what he would say if he was here now. You Silas's only hope.' I see her thinking, I see she knows what I say is true. 'And just one more thing. I am in need of a coat. Spring nights are cold. I got a journey to make and it be a long way to go.'

Hannah go into her bedroom then and come back with an old wool coat. She hand it to me.

'Thank you,' I say. 'This is just fine.'

'You will need a belt to keep it from trailing in the ground.' She go and fetch me a belt and hand it to me. 'Have you eaten?' She ask.

'No, not exactly.' Then I think how it's been a mighty long day since Hetty first come crying through the cottonwoods and I know I got hunger in my belly.

'Sit down,' say Hannah and she bring me a piece of her apple cake and some cheese. She pack some more in paper and tell me this is for my journey.

'I got *The Adventures of Tom Sawyer* with me,' I tell her when I finish eating. And I reach in my bag and pull out the book.

She smile then. 'Good,' she says. 'You are a good pupil, Aiyana, you learn fast and you remember. It will stand you in good stead.'

'Thank you.' I get up from the table. Then I see her go over to the drawer under the gramophone, open it and take something out. It is wrapped in an old cotton sheet. She brings it over to me, unfolds the cotton and I see it is Floyd's hunting knife, there ain't no mistaking it, nor the blood still on it.

'He will pay, Aiyana, he is going pay for what he has done.'

She wrap it back up and fetch her coat and boots. We go up onto the riverbank together and she hurry one way towards the town and jailhouse and I disappear into the wood.

31

I wait and watch, under the shadow of trees until the tyres come screeching down to the river bank, sending the spoonbill and widgeon flying up off the water. I creep out from my hiding place. The moon is up, headlights splinter the night and I see the Sheriff's car pull alongside Floyd's boat. There be a commotion then, lanterns flashing, loud voices echo across the river, boots on the plank. Before long the Sheriff come out with Floyd, hands cuffed behind his back. Mama and Hetty there watching as he taken away. I think at least now they be free of Floyd. At least now justice be done and there is hope for Silas. I ain't hoping Floyd find mercy. I pray the judge tell them to hang him by the neck until he is dead. I thank God for Hannah doing what be right and I pray she find comfort. Then I turn back and find me a hollow, cover myself in leaves and fall into a deep sleep

Grandma come to me in my dreams. I see her walking in the rice fields of the Lakes, sleeping in her old lodge of juniper bark. She call to me and say, 'You have been travelling through a cloud, your sky has been dark, Wild Plum, but soon a great wind will carry you across the land. This is no time to pity ourselves. Let hope wipe away your tears. Let silence make you strong.'

Blossom moon waning. The month is near its end. I been walking four full days now by my reckoning. Me and the river and no one else seeing or listening. I catch its song at the edge of the day, rose light of dawn, blue light of dusk. I walk without rest. Blood and blisters on my feet. Got me some cuts and bruises and thorns from the wild plum. My breath is slow. I ain't even sure now how many days I got left to get to Lyle but I know my days be running out fast. Lyle will already be looking out for me now, waiting there on Canal Street, wondering if I gonna make it. And by my reckoning I ain't gonna make it in time. Nowhere near. A passage on The Verity was my only real hope of reaching Lyle. I think of The Verity and I think of what happened that night. I think of Silas. I am hoping he be set free. I am hoping Sheriff Harper is the good, honest man I think he is.

I do my best to keep the river close by my side. If I follow it, if I get to where it join the Mississippi, then I thinking maybe I can buy me a passage down to the Delta. River is my map. The only one I have. But the map is sometimes hard to follow and I am forced away into the woods by the tangle of bush and tree and nettle and what grows beneath. I am afraid then. Dark thoughts crowd my mind. I think maybe Floyd escape, maybe he is still alive and he come hunting me like he do.

Got no food left to speak of. I eat everything Hannah give me. I am digging roots and picking berries on my way. Take water from the stream where I find it. Hunger twisting in my belly but it ain't nothing like the hunger I got to be following the river out of here. There ain't no way I am turning back now. I rather fall in the river and die through drowning than go back. Only trouble is, I gotta suspicion that I am lost, had no choice but to leave the riverbank again and now I am wandering in the woods and try as I might, I cannot find a way back.

When darkness fall I think the only thing left is to sleep and try again in the morning. I am hungry and the night is cold. I hold Hannah's coat tight around me and lie down in the woods with the whitetail and the possum, green eyes in the blackness, rustle of leaf. I am too weary to make a bed. Lie where I fall, think of grandma on her journey and it give me comfort. She will make it to her people, I know. I know because I saw her in my dream. She will make it and I will make it. Even if I am too late and Lyle is already gone.

I try to conjure grandma to my dreaming but she don't come. My sleep is troubled, head in the river, water in my lungs, and Floyd standing over me. Floyd is chasing at my heels, black shadow towering over me. I cannot breathe. I stumble, fall, he is about to catch me. He is reaching out his arm, his hand clawing at my hair. Then he stop. Shrink away. Floyd disappears. I feel a soft breath on my face and a tongue licking at my hand. See the eyes of the red wolf looking down on me. He lift his paw, then turn and lope off. When I wake I know which way I have to go.

I am up before the songbirds. Spirit of the red wolf on my shoulder. My protector and guide. Above me a fire sky broods red and purple in a crown of thick, black leaves. I walk by instinct on the soft clay of the earth until the fire breaks, until the sky clears. Then in the blue of day, in the trees up ahead, a clearing, and when I reach it, a grassy bank stretching down to the water's edge where sunlight glints on the river. I have found my map and its song rises up on the morning air to whisper in my ear, 'Come down. Listen, listen to my sometime song. It is your song and my song. The song of the wolf and the song of the world.'

Now my path is clear once more, I feel the hunger swell in my belly. Think, if I stop here I might even catch me my breakfast. This is a safe place, a good place to fish in the shallows. I hurry down the bank, sit among the grasses, lay my coat next to me and take off my boots. My skin peels raw with blisters. There is blood on my stockings.

Sun sparks off the water like it do off a crystal, it warms my toes. I long to feel that sun spark off me and I long to soothe my blisters and get my feet in that cool river. I stand up, hitch up my skirt and wade in. I am up to my knees in the river, feet soft in the mud, skirt getting wet. I close my eyes, feel the sun on my face. Think of mama, think of Hetty and Silas and Turner, of what I know and what I don't know. Of what will happen to them. Think the only way I ever know the answer to the questions is if I go back and that ain't possible. Not now. There are some things I may never know and that be the price of my freedom.

Hear the whistle of the train in the distance, beyond the woods. Time I moved on. The day is wasting. I bend to the water to wash the dust from my face. Stand up and shake myself dry. And that's when I see it. Come sailing round the bend in the river. A boat with red sails. Surely I am seeing things. I close my eyes tight, open them again but still it's there. Still. The boat. Red sails coming on and I know that boat anywhere, in any river in the whole wide world. Then I see her, tall in her dark dress, standing on the deck and I cup my hands to my mouth and I start hollering. Hollering for all I am worth, 'Ella! Ella P. Fry!'

I see her arm lift and she start waving. She is waving right back at me and I am waving both arms now and shouting. 'Ella! It's me. Aiyana.'

Then the boat tack across river toward me and I hear Ella calling out my name.

I am sailing down the river with Ella P. Fry, down where I have never been before, where no one but Lyle knows me, knows what I am, knows what I ain't. I am sailing way on down to the Delta, got me a pair of eagle wings, got me a brand new set of lungs, least that's how it feels. Ain't hungering no more. Got me a pen of my very own that Ella give me, and paper, and my book and my pearls. Got the word and the river and the song. Sometimes a river is the song of your soul.